HIDEOUT CANYON

**Center Point
Large Print**

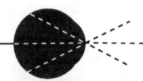

**This Large Print Book carries the
Seal of Approval of N.A.V.H.**

HIDEOUT CANYON

JACK CURTIS

CENTER POINT PUBLISHING
THORNDIKE, MAINE

This Center Point Large Print edition
is published in the year 2010 by arrangement with
Golden West Literary Agency.

The text of this Large Print edition is unabridged.
In other aspects, this book may vary
from the original edition.
Printed in the United States of America
on permanent paper.
Set in 16-point Times New Roman type.

ISBN: 978-1-60285-652-3

Library of Congress Cataloging-in-Publication Data

Curtis, Jack, 1922-
  Hideout canyon / Jack Curtis.
    p. cm.
  ISBN 978-1-60285-652-3 (library binding : alk. paper)
  1. Large type books. I. Title.

PS3505.U866H53 2010
813'.54--dc22

2009032988

=== 1 ===

FORT YUMA, PERCHED ON THE BLUFF IN THE early spring, could be as pretty as a little red heifer in a flower bed at times, and other times, the breeze would die, the temperature rise, and the lifeless atmosphere become as heavy as wet wool.

Locked inside an iron box that would on this day have served to cook a turkey dinner, Wayne Carrol tried his best to imitate a lizard on a rock, crouched motionless, taking an occasional short breath, eyes closed, using as little energy as possible.

What he was being punished for, he couldn't guess, but it wouldn't do to get your blood pressure up over things you didn't know about. The way to survive this day was not to worry, keep your heartbeat at a slow walk, the blood pressure as near zero over zero as possible, respiration short and shallow, the mind blank. Hibernate in the suffocating heat.

Perhaps it was easier for a man in his early forties to control himself. With experience comes patience, and Wayne Carrol had plenty of both. The younger ones who found themselves locked in the hotbox would lose their tempers and waste their strength in rage, beating their hands and feet and heads against the burning iron, cursing the guards, the warden, the nation, and lastly, life itself.

Then there'd be a sullen burial detail.

Without trying, he could hear the chain gang breaking big rocks into little rocks.

If he opened his eyes, he knew he would see a rectangle of pale blue sky, empty of clouds or birds. It wasn't worth watching.

Eight months ago, he'd weighed a hundred eighty pounds; now he'd be lucky to make one forty.

Ribby, a bar of a gray mustache across a visage gaunt and hollow, there was no more fat to fry off him, and he felt dry as a wooden leg.

Best not think of dryness. He wouldn't be given a drink until sunset. You pretend there is no such thing as water, only punishment, and you tell yourself you're tough enough to kick a mule in the butt.

The hardest part was to keep ahold of your thoughts. You get to dreaming, pretty soon you're imagining things, and none of them are any good. You start screaming at monsters that aren't real except in your mind, then you either die or your mind never comes back to your real enemies.

Your real enemies are the guards, the warden, the U.S. Marshal named Shig Radiguet. Don't worry, they're not going anywhere. They're dyin' a day at a time just like everyone else.

Your friends? Frank and Leonardo, they're out.

Then there's Tyson, the boy, ornier'n a rat-tailed horse in fly time. Maybe because his real ma died young. Wouldn't ever listen after that.

Now his stepmom is probably working on him, trying to bend him her way. That *no-good double-crossing knot-headed woman . . . !* Careful now, think on the blue sky for a while, or a long green valley. . . . Forget the woman, forget the give-away. . . .

What do they want? More'n the army payroll. They're smart enough to see it's just money. No, they want to put old Frank and Leonardo in here with me. Make 'em suffer for being good at their line of work, and making the marshals look like what they really are—camp bums hiring out for twenty-four dollars a month and all they can steal. . . . Steady on, Wayne, no need to get all fashed up because a tapeworm of a government man has caught you in a figure eight loop. . . . All you got to do is stay alive one day at a time, and then one day they'll get promoted for accomplishing nothing in their lives and you'll be ridin' up into the cache country . . . free as an eagle. . . .

Young Tyson Carrol might fill out in a few years, might not, depending upon whether he took after his ma or his pa. His ma had been small.

Thin almost to gangliness, his unruly hair like reddish shagbark, he had a certain distinctive determination in the way he walked and an especially fine grace when he was riding. Since he was just sixteen, his slim features weren't fully defined, but he had his dad's cat eyes and set jaw.

Young as he was, still the little lines were already being etched around those brown eyes that seemed as soft as sorghum in July, yet were as sharp and expectant as a sparrow watching a worm hole.

Dressed in clean faded jeans and hickory shirt with a red cotton bandanna around his throat, he rode a big dun mare and, leading a saddled chestnut gelding, was admitted into the prison yard after giving a piece of paper to the guard.

Tethering the horses to a rail in front of the warden's office, he went inside without knocking.

A heavyset guard with oiled curly black hair sitting at a desk looked up. "What do you want, kid?"

"My name's Tyson Carrol. I come to pick up my pa."

"Just a minute." The guard went into the warden's private office, where, even though the building was made of stone, the paunchy warden sweltered almost as much as any unfortunate prisoner who was put in the hotbox.

The sweating warden groaned at the guard's report, put his swollen feet into loose felt slippers, and said, "Send him in."

When Tyson entered, the warden appeared to be studying a printed piece of paper which even Tyson could see was upside down.

After a long false moment of heavy studying and deliberation, the warden looked up at Tyson. "There's conditions," he said. "I explained to your stepma."

"She told me. I don't hold with 'em, I'm just here to take him out," Tyson said abruptly.

"Listen, kid, nobody gives a goddamn what you hold with, you just remember that if your pa gets away with that army payroll, you're goin' to be charged with aidin' and abettin' his escape."

"I ain't in this," Tyson said, not backing up. "I don't work for you or Pa or the army."

"Don't be smart with me!" The warden stood, grease sweating from his jowels. "Your stepma agreed."

"You best find somebody else," Tyson said.

He turned, only to meet the big guard who filled the doorway.

"Well, ain't that a hell of a note." Tyson smiled tightly, and turned back to face the warden.

"You gettin' the idea, kid?" the warden said.

"Well, I do admire the way you put it. You don't say law and order, you don't say justice and the future of America, you just say do it or else."

"Your pa's got a smart mouth like you. You'll see what it got him. You do it my way, the both of you will be free. You wrong me, you'll pay."

"Tell me straight then."

"When your pa goes for the loot, you let me know one way or another. The pardon will go into effect when we have that money back."

"That's what you told my stepmom?"

"It was her idea. She made the deal." The warden grimaced. "She's tougher'n a gypsy horse trader."

Tyson's shining cat eyes were unreadable as he watched the warden. "Suppose that loot is a thousand miles away? Suppose they already spent it?"

"Your pa never had time to spend any of it. We figure he cached it before the split."

"How come you so scratched up about a little money?"

"It's a lot of government money," the warden said carefully.

Tyson never moved a muscle nor twitched an eyelash as he recognized the lie.

Government hacks didn't care dog-do about public money. They just worried how they were going to divide it up amongst themselves.

"Yes, sir," Tyson said.

"You cross me, kid, it'll be the last time, I promise you," the warden said. "I'll see you sweat in hell as long as you can stand it and then double-rig it."

Tyson was thinking he could ride across the river and be in Mexico in about an hour. It might not be any better, but it couldn't be much worse.

The warden was deliberately working outside the law, no doubt in collusion with other lawmen. How could a sixteen-year-old kid win against them?

First get the old man out of here, he thought. You owe him that much. Then run for it.

"You'll find he's changed. Been sick some. Mind wanders."

The boy's cat eyes shone alertly. "You mean for all your special care, he's ailing?"

The warden stood quickly and swung at Tyson's bobbing head, and missed.

"Hold him, Bletcher," the warden growled.

After the guard grabbed Tyson from the back, the warden took his time winding up, and threw as hard a right as he could on a hot day. Tyson, at the last instant, ducked an inch, taking the blow on the high side of his head.

The warden winced as his knuckles gave way, then sat down again as Tyson pretended to sag in the oily guard's arms.

"Haul his old man out of the infirmary and get them both out of here."

"But s'pose they run south?" Bletcher, the guard, asked cautiously.

"They won't," the warden said.

Two guards half carried old Wayne Carrol to the prison yard where Tyson, the top side of his face swelling, stood by the horses waiting.

"Well, you government boys didn't leave much," Tyson said.

"Shut your pan, kid," Bletcher spat. "There's plenty men in here would like a go at you. I kind of fancy you myself."

Tyson's blood suddenly ran cold as he realized just how deep was the corruption in this hellhole.

"Maybe you would like to try," Tyson said, "but first I'd try plucking out your eyes like grapes."

"You little bastard!" The burly guard rushed at Tyson, who quickly slipped under his mare.

"Can you ride, Pa?"

"Hell yes, I can ride," Wayne whispered weakly. "If you'd just remember to dally your chin shut, we could'a been somewhere already."

"It don't seem that keepin' quiet did much for your condition," Tyson said.

"Get moving," Bletcher said.

"You live in Yuma?" Tyson looked at the big guard closely.

"Hell yes, where else could I live?"

"Ever think a crazy kid might look you up some night with an equalizer in his hand?" Tyson asked, staring hard with those burning cat eyes.

"Why, you . . ."

"Might be sooner nor later. . . ." Tyson said.

"Git up." Old Wayne kneed the chestnut, and slumping over the horse's neck, made it out the gate, where he was joined by Tyson.

"Boy," old Wayne croaked, "you ain't got the brains of a grasshopper."

"They ain't goin' to do me like they did you," Tyson said, moving alongside, steadying the older man in the saddle, and walking the horses easy.

"Where we goin'?"

"Home. Your wife's cookin' dinner."

"Can't we just go to a roomin' house?"

"She got you out of there, I don't know why. You sure didn't learn anything."

"If she got me outa there . . ." Wayne muttered, but didn't finish his thought.

"A little home cooking wouldn't hurt, I reckon," he said into the silence.

"She can cook some," Tyson said neutrally.

They rode down the hill, on through a few scattered dusty buildings of the main street, where it was so hot, no one bothered to even look up at the odd pair passing by.

A hundred yards off the street, Tyson led the way to a simple square building built of adobe bricks the same color as the bare dirt around the house.

A mature woman with dark hair and eyes, in her mid-twenties, wearing a simple calico dress and Mexican sandals, came out to help.

From the carefree manner in her movements, it seemed she probably wore no undergarments as a practical concession to the heat.

A strong, vigorous woman with powerful hips and ample breasts, she had a smile on her dark, pleasant face as she went directly to the chestnut gelding.

"Some ganted down," she said, reaching up, putting her arms around Wayne's waist, and lifting him free of the saddle.

"Dim damn it, Kate, put me down," Wayne sputtered helplessly.

"Well, you're not exactly tamed down any," Wayne's wife said. "Can you walk?"

"Course I can walk," Wayne snapped, took a step, swayed, then started to slump.

"C'mon, you old rooster." She grabbed him

again, this time under the arms, and guided him protesting inside to a small bedroom, where she eased him down onto a cot.

"Eight months in there hasn't improved your temper any," she said.

"I'll be fine tomorrow," he said, drifting off.

"Maybe a month of tomorrows," she murmured.

Glancing up, she saw Tyson standing in the doorway, looking at her accusingly.

"What's the matter, Ty?" she asked, already knowing what he would say.

"You made a deal with 'em you can't keep."

"I got him out of there. Another week we'd had to read a Psalm over him."

"But now it's all of us. That warden is a bad one. He don't care nothing about law or justice."

"That makes us even, then." Kate smiled.

"More than a pack of money," Wayne murmured softly, as if dreaming. "It's a treasure, a winner. . . ."

"Maybe they got wind of that," Tyson said. "Likely he talked in his sleep. Maybe they're trickin' you."

"It don't make a never mind," Kate said, going to the kitchen stove, where a pot of rich stew simmered. "I got him out of there."

"Course, he thinks you put him in there."

"He can't! I made a mistake maybe, but how did I know he'd hang back and fort up while his pals ran off and left him?"

When he awakened, towards dark, Wayne

couldn't remember where he was. He thought maybe they'd put him down in the hole again, but this place had a bed and it smelled clean. He tried to get up, but his legs wouldn't support him and he groaned as he fell back.

"Wayne, *mi amor*," Kate said anxiously, "you awake?"

"You double-crossin' hellcat," he growled.

"Save your strength." She smiled. "Let me give you a little supper, make you forget what ails you."

"Loaded with carpet tacks, I suppose," Wayne said, as she put a tray on the bed with a bowl of stew, fresh-baked bread, and a bottle of warm beer.

"Dig deep, puppy on bottom." She grinned, spooning up the stew.

"I can feed myself," he said, taking the spoon away from her.

"We'll talk tomorrow," she murmured when he finished and lay back on the cot.

"You better have an interesting yarn to tell."

"I'll think of something." She nodded and took the tray out to the kitchen.

U.S. Marshal Shig Radiguet, dressed in tan twill trousers and a tan shirt with the sleeves rolled up, sat on the edge of the warden's desk, and helped himself to the cigar box.

"You think they'll follow through?" Shig rasped through his nose, which had been broken years ago by a cowboy with a deceptively fast left hook.

"Why not? I don't think any of 'em got past the flyleaf of the first grade primer."

"It's a long chance. But if he leads us to Frank McCloud and Leonardo Fajardo, we're halfway home."

"And the money. I want half of that," the warden said.

"You don't get half if you don't ride with me," the huge marshal said, deliberately blowing smoke in the warden's fat face and grinding the cigar out on the varnished desktop.

"You know I can't ride far," the warden protested. "I let him loose for you."

"Suppose you send Bletcher?"

"What's his cut?"

"Write it off as vacation with pay."

"Sixty thousand two ways?" the warden asked.

"I'm takin' half. The rest is up to you." Radiguet grinned, showing a broken front tooth.

"Just so we have it straight. Fifty-fifty is the cut."

"Soon as the old bastard can ride, I'll be on his tail."

"Don't underestimate him, Shig, he's tough as iron bars."

The warden marched off to the door and called into the other office. "Bletcher!"

"Yes, sir." The short, broad-shouldered guard came to the doorway.

"Come in. You know Marshal Radiguet. You're going on special assignment with him."

"Yes, sir," Bletcher said carefully, his mind spinning, trying to find an answer before he lost the advantage.

"Get ready to ride. Take a good horse from the stable, and pack no more than necessary."

"Is there a bonus?" Bletcher asked softly.

"I'm giving you a few days off. You like it here so much, I can find somebody else," the warden said angrily, staring at the barrel-shaped man.

"I don't want to lose my seniority," Bletcher said, deciding to play stupid.

"I'll fix it so you add on an extra year," the warden said.

"Yes, sir. An extra year will make me ten years and eight and a half months."

"Goddamnit, Bletcher, can't you think of something besides a pension you might get after forty years' service?"

"It's part of the job, sir," Bletcher said dully. "I don't do this work for the weekly wage."

"Get ready to travel with Marshal Radiguet and do what he tells you. Understood?"

"Yes, sir. But is it legal?"

"Of course it's legal. I'm making it legal."

"Yes, sir. Just give me a little note to that effect."

"Good Lord!" the warden stormed in exasperation, and wrote a quick note. "I can see why you're worried about a pension thirty years away."

"Yes, sir. I've learned it's better to stay inside the system."

17

"Draw a six-gun and a repeating rifle from the armory, and plenty of ammunition. Take whatever food you want to carry along from the commissary, and don't ask me for any more goddamned chits!"

"Yes, sir. I'll see to it." Bletcher made a thin-lipped smile. Now he knew it was something big, and the warden was too shaky to hide his greed.

He would take a bonus somewhere along the line, one way or another, even if he had to grab the warden between his two hands and squeeze him like a big sponge. He would get out of the sinkhole once and for all, and let the pension be damned.

"What are you waiting for?" The warden glared at him.

"I was just thinking, sir—"

"Get out of here," the warden said nervously. "Go beat up somebody."

"Yes, sir." Bletcher turned like a barrel on casters and left.

As soon as the door closed, the warden whispered fiercely, "The son of a bitch is already thinking of how to grab it all for himself."

"Make it fifty-five, forty-five"—Radiguet smiled— "and I'll take care of him for you."

"Done. By God, done!" The warden gripped the marshal's beefy hand.

The adobe hut was quiet in the twilight. Young Tyson sat on a bench on the shady side, wrapping a length of wet rawhide piggin' string around the grips of an old Army Colt he'd bought off an Indian for a dollar. It was rusted, the barrel pitted, and the nipples crusted with misfires, but he had managed to knock the steel barrel wedge free that held it all together, so he could clean each part with sand and coal oil, and even though the grips were broken and a couple of the chambers doubtful, it was a hundred percent better than it was when he bought it. He'd likely fire it tomorrow with a light charge to be on the safe side.

"What are you going to do with that thing?" Kate asked, coming out the door.

"Shoot it."

"Shoot what?"

"The warden and his oily guard."

"You don't do that, Tyson," she said. "We'll lose the whole shebang, you start thinking that way."

"You goin' to watch Dad through the night?" Tyson asked, settling the six-gun in its battered holster on his hip, then practicing a fast draw.

"Better I take the cot by the door." She nodded.

"I'll be down at the barn," Tyson said, twirling the old .45 with his finger through the brass trigger guard.

The velvet evening cooling the parched terrain was welcome, and no one thought of guarding the house from inside or out.

A couple of dogs howled at the moon as it went overhead, and towards dawn the roosters announced their dominions, and about daylight,

Kate stirred, and, half-asleep, looked in the bedroom.

What was wrong?

It took her a minute to puzzle it out.

"Tyson!" she yelled. "The old devil's gone!"

= 2 =

TYSON CHECKED THE OUTHOUSE JUST TO BE sure, but Wayne wasn't there, and when he discovered the chestnut was gone, there was no doubt.

"Oh, that *cabrón*!" Kate wailed. "How can he do this to me?"

"He's a fox. He learned to be a sneak from them Paiutes he lived with. I was sleepin' not ten feet from that chestnut and he never made a nicker nor stamped his hoof."

"But he seemed so sick. Hell, he's down to nothin' but bones and balin' wire." Kate's broad face was dark and drawn with worry.

"You can't trust him," Tyson said shortly. "He learned actin' when he was a kid with a travelin' troupe doing *Uncle Tom's Cabin*. He knows everything except how to make an honest livin'."

"He couldn't make up that *debilidad*," she insisted, reverting to her mother's Spanish.

"Reckon he did. What you goin' to tell Radiguet?"

"Nothin'. We're hightailin' it outa here, *ya pronto*! You got two minutes to pack."

20

"I was packed last night," Tyson said, and went to saddle the horses, thinking he was stuck with a fool woman you couldn't trust, chasin' his fool father you couldn't trust either.

Thinking on it, he decided he'd play the game his way if that's how they wanted it. He wouldn't trust them, and if they trusted him, they were crazy as June bugs in January.

Kate changed into riding clothes, then packed a valise, a carpetbag, and a big canvas war bag.

"I'm not waiting for Shig Radiguet or you either," Tyson said, standing in the doorway watching the pile of bags grow. "The war bag is all your horse can carry."

"Damn it, Tyson, unbend a little." Kate turned to face him, her handsome face flushed with the feverish rush. "I've got to have some clothes."

"I said I'm leavin'. I got enough clothes to keep the flies off, and I reckon you better think along those same lines."

"Damn it, if you were my kid . . ." She glowered.

"If you was my ma, you'd been buried ten years." He spat on the dirt floor, walked out, and mounted his big dun mare.

"All right!" She rushed out with the canvas sack. "Let me tie this on behind, and we're leavin'. . . . Damn kid . . ."

After the bag was secured, she swung aboard the bay and said, "Lead on. For sure, a smart kid like you knows the way."

21

"He'd oughter cross the river and ride into Sonora to rest up, but he's too twisted to do the best thing. The next smartest thing is he'd ride west to California and enjoy himself."

"More likely he'd cross the desert north so he could enjoy the sufferin'," she said.

"It's a possibility I considered, but he's after something different. It ain't the army payroll money so much as the treasure he's found somewhere or just remembered from a dream he had."

"That could be anywhere."

"I'm bettin' he'll try to find Frank and Leonardo."

"Why?"

"Because it don't make any sense at all except they was all ridin' together when Radiguet took him."

"You're just guessing," she said.

"It's in New Mexico. Has to be," Tyson said.

"Why?"

"They stuck up the paymaster just north of Tres Cruces."

"That was a year ago."

"You can ride for California. Likely you'd do well there," Tyson said, kneeing the mare down the trail to the east.

"Wait, damn it, I'm a full partner in this fracas."

God knows you started it with your meddlin', Tyson thought as he set the big dun to an easy gallop, but Dad ain't no better. He's just as much a do-gooder as she is, and they're both losers.

The sun broke loose in the east as they cleared the last abandoned shack of Yuma and rode along the Gila River Trail east with the sun in their eyes.

"Reckon we made it out before anybody saw us?" Kate asked, worried now that they'd wasted too much time packing.

"Wasn't no one around leastways," Tyson said, trying to picture how it would go when Radiguet came out smellin' around. He might just send some old bum, pretending to want a crust of bread or something. That probably wouldn't happen till midmorning. By then their tracks should be covered. If he was Radiguet, he'd figure the whole passel had run for Mexico, if only because Kate was half-Mexican, where she got her temper. Her gringo professor daddy was probably an abolitionist or a Mormon, the way she liked to meddle in other folks' business.

"I suppose he's pretty mad at us to run off like this," Kate said, hating to admit that her man had some justification.

"I never meddled in his affairs," Tyson said.

"But you back-sass him."

"No, ma'am, talkin' some cold iron horse sense into his dreamworld is all I try to do. Why don't we have a nice ranch right now on a running stream with a lot of bottomland grass and a herd of cattle and a cavvy of first-class horses?"

"He's always said he'd do it," she said.

"He's always dreamin' on it, but anybody else

his age has already taken the good valleys, and are settin' back in their rockin' chairs, eatin' apple pie and watchin' the hired hands work."

"He'll do it."

"He won't do it if he spends all his time robbin' payrolls and such."

"He gets along with folks real well."

"Meanin' I don't. Well, I don't need to take any dust off anybody, and don't intend to. I'll get the damned ranch, but it won't be by tryin' to help every damned puke on the trail, or throwin' in with a couple losers who are always down on their luck. How come if he gets along so well with everybody worshipin' him for goin' broke and spendin' time in the pen, why don't he run for governor or something?"

"He'd do good." She nodded.

"No, he wouldn't. Hell's afire, everybody'd vote for the two-faced slicker. They wouldn't vote for somebody that'd treat 'em square."

"Why not?"

"It's the nature of the pukes. They like to give their money away to their top liars!" Tyson snorted cynically.

"All right, so he won't never be a politician," she said, closing the subject. "But he could be a teacher if he'd study on it some with me. Or he could be a preacher."

"No, he'd have to go out and rob a bank every day just to keep all the poor folks comin' in for his message. He wouldn't never pass the collection plate, he'd have it the other way, for sure. Everybody just draws out all they want and says 'amen, brother.'"

"You figure him ·pretty close," Kate laughed. "I reckon his ears are burning right now."

"Not him," Tyson muttered, pulling up.

"What . . . ?" Kate asked, puzzled.

"He's turned off," Tyson said, seeing the sun had come up towards noon already. "He's tired and hungry."

"How do you know?"

Tyson turned back until he found the telltale hoof-prints, then studied their angle where they left the trail toward the right.

"He's gone over to the river," he said. "That is, if you can trust anything at all. Come slow."

He knew he'd lose the prints as soon as they left the trail, because cattle and goats and mustangs had traveled over the loose desert earth, and you couldn't tell one from another.

Radiguet had to come up with a cold trail.

Course, he could telegraph ahead and ask for word of them, but knowing that, they could go around the towns.

At least for this day, Tyson Carrol decided he wouldn't worry about Shig Radiguet. He'd worry about running down his dad before he got himself hurt.

The fact was, the early dew on the trail had

revealed tracks that Tyson recognized easily enough although he decided not to share that information with Kate.

He'd had the chestnut shod just the week before and watched the blacksmith break open a keg of new iron shoes, and after trimming down the hooves with his steel biters, and smoothing them off with his rasp, all the time cussing the dog that kept darting in and eating the hoof trimmings like they was candy, nailed on the new black iron shoes, bent the nails, and remarked at the three *B*s, one at each tip of the shoe and the third centered at the front.

"Birmingham Iron," the smith had said. "I guess they're comin' back."

It was those *B*s that were marking the chestnut's trail, not the letter itself, but the odd indentations in each track.

The old man had been traveling slower after he'd cleared town. Maybe he was saving the horse, maybe he was saving himself.

He sure as hell must've wanted to leave for a powerful reason, as if another day of rest and some soup might keep him from payin' off some widder woman's mortgage off in Wyoming or Montana.

Setting a sight on a giant boulder surrounded by yuccas, he kneed the mare and figured it was as good a guess as any. If he missed, he'd just go downriver or upriver. For sure the old man would go to water just like a goose.

Kate followed behind, annoyed that she wasn't running things, and mystified that Tyson should be so trail-wise, just like his papa.

Old Wayne Carrol, who never had thought of himself as old, was feeling drained out and so dizzy, he was losing his bearings about an hour after sunup. He'd made good time out of Yuma because the wagon trail was easy to follow and the chestnut was sensible.

He'd drifted out of Yuma soft as a feather, going barefoot out of the house and leading the chestnut out of the stable where the boy was sleeping. He'd made his plan the night before and had an idea where the food was, and his canteen and guns. Couldn't let on to those things when you're supposed to be knocking at the pearly gates, but he survived by knowing just where the necessities could be found in a hurry.

Hated to leave them like that. Good-hearted, contrary-headed Kate wanted to nurse somebody. Should get her with a baby and settle her forward ways. Anyways, that'd be later, if ever. Now was the time to get free and see if that boy had the sense of a cricket or was he just noisy and worthless.

If he could learn just to trust folks, not all folks, just some folks, then he could probably have some kind of a happy life, but if he never trusted nobody and went around with a chip on his shoulder all the time, no doubt somebody'd knock it off and put him down for good. You had to have some folks around that cared to be friendly.

What the boy needed most was to know he could win. Not win by being the meanest dog in the ring, but win by patience and ideas and the help of friends.

If I could just teach him that much, I'd call myself a successful father, he thought tiredly. Maybe I can, maybe I can't. Whatever way it goes, though, he gets a chance.

You could count on that Kate to stick her nose into the porcupine's butt sure as hell. She'd had that "holy Mary Guadalupe" look on her face that meant she'd sold him out again for his own good, but this time, he wasn't waiting for her to deliver him to no hotbox nor give his money back to the government, nor see that his years were spent peacefully behind bars.

He didn't much like tricking her like that, but he couldn't see much choice. Once he found Frank and Leonardo and secured the cache, then he could maybe stand her if she'd stay in the kitchen or go back to teachin' while he rode the rimrock.

He grinned at himself, his seamed face woefully tired and gray, but still he could smile at the cards life dealt out to him.

Now he was just plumb tuckered, and with any luck at all, the kid would be down in Sonora with his stepmom, asking which way he went.

He smiled again, thinking that the Mexicans would always point off somewhere and say *allá!* because they wanted you to be happy. It didn't make any difference what you asked, they'd always say, "Yes, over there!"

Even Kate, being half-Mex, wouldn't be able to dent that tradition. "Yes, over there!"

Alli allá! Aquí, acá!

He smelled smoke, that dry, acrid smoke of burning desert fuel; whether ironwood, mesquite, yucca, or dead cactus, it was always a sharp, clean, tasty odor, and he tested the wind to see where it was coming from.

Beyond that big boulder. Yes, there was a granddaddy mesquite just beyond. Probably was on a rise above the river. Anyway there'd be water and food.

Slumping over the saddle, he let the chestnut pick its way toward the river, where there had to be a little shade, and if there was nothing to eat, he'd share the cornbread and sowbelly he'd taken from the shack in the night. Water. Rest. Eat, and *allá!*

Somewhere along the line he'd have to cut off and follow the Salt Creek Trail towards Tucson, but that'd be tomorrow at least.

He found a simple ramada made of brush laid on poles, with a few rocks piled around it to maybe keep the rattlers out, and not far off were pens made of woven sticks where the goats were kept at night. The river was mostly sand, but there was a pool not far from the ramada, enough to water the goats and keep the family clean.

He stopped the chestnut at some distance from the ramada so they could look him over before taking a shot at him and croaked, *"Hola, a la casa. Tienes agua?"*

A small, muscular man wearing only a pair of ragged pants moved out of the shade and called back, *"Ven!"*

"Gracias," Wayne said, and kneed the chestnut into a walk that showed he was harmless enough.

Goats of every size and color moved about on thin legs, and Wayne wondered how the goats and the family could live off each other since neither had much of anything.

He dismounted and led the chestnut to the water. *"Con permiso,"* he said, before letting the horse drink.

"Sí, propio, andale," the short, heavyset Mexican said, watching.

After watering the horse, Wayne tied him in the shade of the mesquite, loosened his leathers, and then moved inside the shady ramada.

"Sientese."

The Mexican was probably half Yaqui Indian from the sharp, high voice he used, shrilling the syllables.

"Gracias, señor."

After that, the family, composed of a wife who stayed in her own corner where the cook fire was, and five or six naked children, offered him what they had, which was just about what he expected. Goat stew with plenty of *chiles serranos*, and *tortillas de maíz*, which no doubt had started out as yellow corn being ground into flour on the gray metate by the fire. But as a treat, the man offered him a tortilla wrapped around some fried meat.

"Víbora." The man smiled as Wayne looked inside the rolled-up tortilla.

"Increíble," Wayne said, tasting the rattlesnake and finding it delicious. *"Que sabrosa!"*

He'd thought it might be a gila monster or an iguana, both of which he savored more than rattlesnake, but the rattlesnake was pure energy.

"Muy fuerte." The Mexican grinned and clapped his left hand over his right elbow, making a fist, and the sign of potency.

"I don't have a need," Wayne replied in Spanish with a grin.

"You are Don Wayne?" the Mexican asked.

"How'd you guess?" Wayne shook his head in wonder.

"Everybody knows you are a friend."

"Please say nothing."

"I would die first," the Mexican said strongly.

Bull-shouldered Shig Radiguet, sullen, sadistic, and usually alert for the big chance, slept late that morning, having had too much tequila in the border cantina, and too much action upstairs with the fat lady who had looked a helluva lot more romantic downstairs with her clothes on.

His head throbbed like a tuba keeping time to "Yankee Doodle." His mouth was dry and caked with his decayed excesses, his small bulging eyes were red-rimmed and painful. His hands trembled as he sought his pants.

"No quieres mas?" The fat lady smiled coquettishly at him, which made him run to the balcony and retch, saliva drooling from his mouth.

"Jesus God, I promise never again. Never never never ever again. Please, mercy."

He couldn't remember where he'd put his horse, and thought for a while that some son of a bitch had stolen it, until the old mozo said he'd taken it over to the livery for the night. The mozo expected a tip for the service, and to make the gringo feel good, he raised his right arm and clapped his hand over the elbow. *"Eres muy fuerte, sí!"*

He knew his wallet would be empty. Either the bartender, the mozo, or the whore would have cleaned it out. For that he was mistaken—they had left him eight dollars from the forty he'd had the day before.

Don't worry, mister, he told himself. There's sixty thousand out there at the edge of town just waitin' for me to cash it in.

By midmorning, he could hold a cup of coffee

down, and then he tried the ham and eggs. Fine. The ache in his head was slowly withdrawing. The desire to hurt someone was increasing.

Not that he thought of it in that way. He went by his feelings. If he felt like eating, he ate. If he felt mean, he looked for a fight; if he felt horny, he hired a whore; and if he felt anxious, he would bare his teeth and squint his little hog eyes, and hunt for trouble.

. . . Where was that half-breed nauch? She'd promised to get word to him as soon as the old man was ready to ride. Well, then, maybe he wasn't ready just yet. Maybe the hotbox was a little extra for a thin-gutted butthead. Lots of times the real dumb ones, the loonies, died in the box because they thought they were supposed to. You put 'em in a pile of ice, they'd freeze to death for the same reason.

The ones that wasn't crazy, they could handle a full day of the hotbox if they didn't panic.

What the hell's the difference? he thought. The old man lived through it. All he really needed was plenty of water. Beer would be better, but water would bring him back. Body needs water, he thought, even though he hadn't drunk a drop of water for fifteen years. He drank coffee, beer, and hard liquor mixed with lime juice, but he had no taste for water.

Once Carrol had the juices back in his body, he'd be tough as an old jackrabbit, and he'd be running like a big bluetick hound dog had smelt his butt.

That was the trouble. If he figured out the trap, he was plenty lobo, plenty bronco, plenty goddamned polecat.

Walking across the street to the cantina, he found the old mozo and put a dime in his open hand. "Go out there to the shack on the left. The one with the corral. Ask the woman for breakfast, or work, or something. Look around. Then come back here."

"*Sí, señor.*"

In an hour, the old mozo returned to find Shig Radiguet working on his third beer.

"Christ, you took long enough. What'd she say?"

"*No está.*"

"Not there?"

"*Sí, señor.*"

"You sure you got the right house?"

"The door is open. The horses are gone."

"How long?"

"*No se. Un rato, quién sabe.*"

"That bitch, when I catch up with her I'm going to fire up a red-hot poker and make it sizzle."

"*Corazón!*" the fat whore cried out in greeting as she came down the stairway.

"Your damned beer is too warm to drink," the burly marshal growled, and leaving his glass half-empty, walked out without paying.

"*Pinche gringo,*" the bartender said, patting his left elbow with the palm of his right hand in the Mexican gesture meaning cheapskate.

Radiguet found Bletcher in the prison office, half-asleep in the swivel chair behind the desk.

"Rise up, we're leaving." Shig smacked his fist on the desktop.

"I been waitin'," Bletcher groaned, waking up and stretching his long arms. "I'm pretty near ready."

"All you need is your guns," Shig Radiguet growled.

═══ 3 ═══

RETURNING TO THE MAIN TRAIL, WAYNE Carrol rode on steadily. The rest and the solid meal lifted his spirits, and he felt some strength returning to his long ramrod body.

Late in the afternoon he saw the squared-off rock and adobe shapes shimmering in the heat waves across a long, dry flat. The stage stop, known as Gila Bend, marked the turn of the river north, and he could follow it on up to Fort McDowell or he could cut easterly across the god-awful rocky *mala país*, waterless and torrid, not to save time so much as to lose whatever pursuit might be following.

Longing for a hot supper and a bed off the ground, he almost went on in, but he decided it wasn't worth the chance.

Instead he turned off on a little rise of broken shale that would betray no tracks, passed up a dry coulee, and cut the riverbed a mile shy of Gila Bend.

Watering the horse and filling his canteen, he

sighted in his landmarks, shrugged his shoulders, and bore due east.

Dusty brown and rocky, old game trails led him on until his shadow was long and the sun settled toward the western rim of the desert like a bucket of burning oil.

It was Apache country, but the Apaches didn't like it any better than he did. They'd stay with the water if they could, because that's where the loot was, ranches to plunder, Mexican traders to raid, wagon trains to burn.

There was nothing out in these rock-cursed barrens to interest an Indian on the warpath.

Making a dry camp, he chewed on some dried goat, which tasted some better than he'd expected, and let the chestnut snuffle through the rocks, looking for a tuft of grass or a few windblown seeds. He'd feed the big horse well tomorrow, but he'd have to go dry a while longer.

Wayne rested until the nearly full moon rose and the stars were out on their enormous stage, then he tightened his leathers again, swung aboard the chestnut, and kneed him into a safe walk, dropping down into dry barrancas, coming up over rock-plated hogbacks, yet keeping the moon in his eyes and the North Star on his left shoulder.

When the moon was overhead, he picked the three lined-up stars of Orion following after and used them as his guide.

It was slow going, but it could be no other way,

even as the heat of the rocks dissipated into the cool darkness.

Be pure uncut hell, he thought, if a man was set afoot out here. Worse'n the hotbox in the Yuma pen, because your brains would addle under the sun and the crazy jumble of broken rock, and you'd know there was no end to it.

This time of the year the sun would rise a few degrees north of east, he decided, and watched the faint glow slowly erase the stars. He'd been cat-napping through the night, but it hadn't rested his weary bones because of the constant ups and downs and turns this way and that.

Luckily the horse was smart enough to figure out the general direction they were going and kept a steady course in spite of the zigs and zags of the broken country.

As the pale yellow light flooded over the scalped hills, there was a new lively freshness in the air for a few minutes as if it might have just rained, but there had been no rain to speak of for a hundred years or more. Only a few cacti and giant saguaros with their arms extended to the sky as if imploring for mercy could be called verdant. Even the tiny leaves of the creosote bush were nearly white and brittle.

The chestnut was tired, but he still walked along steadily, trusting that his rider knew where he was going and that there would be water and grass there when they arrived.

His ears pricked up at a strange sound some-where up ahead and Wayne Carrol murmured, "Steady, boy, what do you hear?"

Without pausing, Wayne loosened the rifle under his leg so it would come out of the scab-bard if he needed it in a hurry. Then he lifted the Army Colt .45 from its holster to check its loads. Whatever the horse heard wasn't natural to the rock barrens, and there wasn't enough moisture out here to carry a ringtailed cat, let alone a deer or puma.

He'd know when he came over the next rise. There was no smell of smoke, not a trace of an Apache or anything else except the desiccated droppings of a kangaroo rat on a rocky perch.

Mighty fine country, he thought with a faint smile, for a man tired of city life. No noise except the vaguest of songs from the tiny desert wren. Only traffic would be the shadow of a raven passing overhead.

From the top of the rise he could see a red butte far to the east, and let out a little sigh of relief. The butte was his landmark and he'd hit it dead center.

"Three or four hours," he murmured to the chestnut, whose ears were still up, pointing this way and that.

It was a human voice sobbing softly. A man. Where?

Wayne grimaced. Off in the distance was the goal that he'd ridden all night to reach, but there was someone in this tangle of rock slabs that needed help.

He stopped the horse and stood in the stirrups, peering down into the next barranca, which looked like all the rest of them.

He cupped his hands to his mouth and hollered, "Hello there!"

The land was so long, there wasn't an echo.

But the strange weeping ceased. Someone had heard his voice.

"Where . . . are . . . you?" he called again.

"We don't know. . . ." came a croaking cry from far off to the right in a mess of boulders.

"Over here . . ." another voice sounded weakly.

"Here!" came the first voice. "Help!"

"Take it easy, I'm comin'," he called, and turned the gelding to the right and worked through the slabbed rock, staying on high ground until he could see two people huddled in the shade of a pile of overhanging rocks.

He let the chestnut pick his own way down the slope, and when he reached the shelter, the pair crawled out on hands and knees, their faces lifted, imploring.

"Water . . . please . . ." a big, hawk-faced woman croaked dryly.

The man tried to speak, but couldn't find his voice, and used his eyes to beg with.

The man wore a black suit, shiny and threadbare with age; the woman's black muslin dress was sweated out orange under the arms and breasts. On her feet were the brogans of a farmer, and perched on top of her short-cut hair was a round straw hat, dyed black, with two artificial cherries on the hatband.

Loosening the canteen, Wayne gave the woman a small drink and forced it out of her hands as she tried to drink it dry.

"Little by little," he said patiently, and gave the man a tad extra.

"Thank God we've been saved," the man declared. His face was burned a bright red and blistered near the hairline. The woman sat down, and Wayne gave her another sip of water and another for the man.

"Lost?" he asked.

"Oh, he's a smart one," the big woman said hatefully, her eyes on the man. " 'Take the shortcut,' he said."

"We had to do something," the man said weakly. "The wagon train wouldn't carry us anymore. Just left us out in the desert to die."

"I never heard of a wagon master that hard," Wayne said.

"He feared the word of Nariz the Prophet," the man said defensively. "He said if I preached anymore, he'd cut us adrift, and there is no way I'm going to back down on my religion."

Crazy, thought Wayne. Hopeless case. Joined a sect as crazy as he already was and just couldn't shut up about it.

"You have a wagon?"

"We started off from Independence with a wagon and four horses," the woman said. "By the time we come to Lordsburg, we had two horses and a two-wheel cart."

"The Prophet is trying our faith," the man said.

"Are you a believer?" The woman stared at Wayne's weather-lined, dust-grimed visage.

"I'm a believer in live and let live."

"You want to go to hell, you just keep on thinking that way. You want to go to the marble mansion of the white robes, you better listen to me."

"Mister, we're moving. I'll lead you on over to a ranch I know of, and you can work out your time from there on."

"I can't walk," the woman said.

"Me neither," the man said.

"Me neither." Old Wayne cracked a smile. "Not in these boots leastwise."

"We could ride double," the woman said.

"The horse is tired. He ain't got that much left in him," Wayne said. "You ride. Your man and me can each hold on to a stirrup, that'll be some help, and we'll get pointed towards Butte Ranch."

"I can't," the man whined, refusing to get to his feet.

"You goin' to have to or go visit your prophet," Wayne said. "That sun will be a killer in an hour or so."

"You're not as worn-out as us," the woman said, accusingly.

"Look there, see yonder that red butte." Wayne pointed. "Head for that butte and you'll find a stage stop and a ranch at the base of it."

"I can't do it," the man said. "Help us in the name of God and the Prophet!"

"Mister, I done give you my water. If you can't go it, I'll send somebody out for you with some extra horses."

"You'd just go off and leave us to die?" the woman cried out bitterly.

"No, ma'am. I offered you the only choice possible. There is no other way, because the horse is about done in. He can carry one, but he can't carry double. Now, if you'll understand that much, and you want to come along with me, let's be moving before that sun scorches us right out of the skillet."

"You see," the man said to his wife, "they're all just alike."

"Amen," the woman said, her eyes bright.

"If you're goin' with me, we better get travelin'," Wayne offered one more time, unable to just leave them out here in this pitiless wasteland despite their obstinancy.

"We'll do it our own way according to the Prophet," the man said, eyeing the woman, who nodded.

"Very well." Wayne gave up. "I'll send help soon as I can."

As he turned to mount up, he caught sight of a flashing movement off to his right quarter where the woman was standing, but when the rock smacked the back of his head, he never knew what hit him.

Young Tyson Carrol looked at the empty-faced Mexican goatherder, turned, and picked up a bun of horse manure under the mesquite. It was dry outside and might be a week old, but when he broke it open, it was still moist. He sniffed at it briefly, and looked up at Kate.

"He's told the man not to talk, but he was here maybe three hours earlier."

"Dime," Kate said.

The short goatherder shrugged. Turning away, he walked stolidly into the ramada and lay down on a blanket, ignoring Tyson and Kate.

"That's it," Tyson said. "He was here. What else do you want to know?"

"Where he went."

"I told you—if he went east, he's aiming over towards Tres Cruces."

"We've got to find him before that," Kate said.

"Why?" Tyson asked, kneeing the dun mare forward.

"Because he's not well."

"Hell, he can run both of us into the ground with an anvil strapped on his back."

"Maybe he'll rest up at Gila Bend," Kate said,

her strong features composed, as if she were thinking ahead.

"We'll see," Tyson said doubtfully, and kicked the dun to an easy gallop.

They came into Gila Bend before noon. A stage was waiting for a change of horses. The driver and a couple passengers were inside the station having an early dinner.

The driver, a short-legged, gray-haired mule skinner with a tobacco-stained white beard, glanced up as they sat at the plank table across from him.

"Hot out, ain't it?" the driver said, sociably.

"You coming down from McDowell?" Kate asked, before Tyson could say something smart.

"That's right, ma'am. Next stop Yuma."

"Seen a lone rider?" Kate smiled. "An old rannie on a chestnut gelding?"

"Nope. Passed a troop of soldier boys riding north, that's about it. Always like to see them boys out ridin'. Means they're not all settin' around waitin' for news of a massacree!" the driver laughed.

A shapeless, lank-haired woman came and mopped the plank in front of Kate and Tyson, looking at them questioningly.

"Just make us up a sack of roast beef sand-wiches," Tyson said. "We can eat on the trail."

"Going north?" the old driver asked.

"Maybe," Tyson said, "maybe not."

"Your brother's some salty for his age, ma'am."
The driver smiled at Kate.

"That's the way they are nowadays." Kate nodded.

"Likely somebody'll knock it out of him before too long," the driver continued, a grin on his face, but with hard, mean eyes.

"Anytime you're ready," Tyson said clearly, hitching at his gun belt.

"I'm ready," Kate said, rising quickly.

"I didn't mean you," Tyson said, his cat eyes fixed on the old driver, his right hand poised above the mended grips of the Colt.

"Don't take me wrong, son," the bearded man said. "I was just meaning a man gets along a lot better bein' sociable."

"I ain't arguin' with you," Tyson said, relaxing, and out of pure wickedness he added, "And I ain't her brother."

Kate walked strongly after him on out the door, leaving the old driver glaring meanly after them.

"If he were mine, I'd club that out of him," he said in a low voice to a drummer sitting beside him.

"Now, what's on your mind, Tyson?" Kate asked, once they were clear.

"We ain't seen his track in the last mile. Means he turned off. Didn't want to be seen. You want to try ridin' across that hellish country or stay on the trail?"

"Do you know the way?"

"No. I heard him say it could be done from here to Red Butte Station, but he never showed me."

"Better to take the long way around," Kate said, realizing now that Wayne was playing for keeps.

Tyson led the way by half a step up the canyon trail, trying to estimate the number of miles against the time it took to get to Fort McDowell. Then from McDowell on around to Red Butte.

Near the fort itself, a small village had sprung up to serve the soldiers as well as the stage and freight traffic. It wasn't much more than a rooming house, restaurant, blacksmith shop, and a small mercantile, but it suited Kate fine.

Not used to a hard day's riding, she was stiff, sore, and tired.

She had no doubts that they would catch up with her reluctant husband, even if they arrived a day or two late.

Wayne had something on his mind, and whatever it was would take a day or two, maybe a month, to fix.

They had mentioned the gray-mustached man riding a chestnut gelding, but no one had seen him.

"Ten to one, he'll think he's clear at Red Butte and hole up for a little rest," Kate suggested to Tyson while they had a light supper.

"Likely you're right, ma'am," Tyson replied mildly.

She looked at him curiously. Why had he all of sudden become such a darlin' boy?

"Tired?" she asked.

"Some." He nodded.

"You wouldn't be playing no tricks on your good old stepmom, would you?" she murmured with a fixed smile.

"Dad has the bag of tricks. I'm just bein' agreeable."

"It don't suit you," she said.

"Likely not. I been made out of pegged-out rawhide, and can't do nothing about it, even if I try." He nodded.

"Keep trying, Tyson." She smiled for real this time, her white teeth flashing. "You'd be surprised how happy you can be."

"Such a thing ain't in my nature, ma'am," Tyson said solemnly.

"It's something you can change." She patted his shoulder. "You just keep doing what you're doing now, and you'll be president of America right soon."

"Is that all it takes, just bein' agreeable?"

"Well, it don't hurt to have the banks backin' you up," she laughed.

"What do you suppose he was talkin' about when he was ravin' about the treasure?" Tyson put in mildly.

"The army payroll likely."

"Payroll don't sound like treasure to me," Tyson said thoughtfully. "Treasure's something bigger'n a payroll, something you dig up. Something you find that nobody else knows about. He—" Tyson coughed, and seemed to catch himself.

"He what?" she asked directly.

"I forgot," Tyson said. "It was just a dumb idea anyway. We both know he wants to straighten out Frank and Leonardo, and buy some ranch down in Mexico."

"He's so damned afraid of talkin' sense, he won't even say where that is," Kate said bleakly. "He acts like I'd run it down were he to mention there was snow around eighteen feet deep in July, or the other way, if it was a slab of burned rock five by ten miles with only dew for water, he'd think I'd downgrade it as bein' a trifle dry for beef."

"He does hang himself with words, don't he?" Tyson smiled, his long face losing the hound-dog mournfulness, although she noticed there was no joy to be seen in those deep-set cat eyes.

"Reckon we better figure on an early start," Tyson said, standing and yawning. "Your bunk all right?"

"Fine, Tyson, thanks," Kate said, grateful that the boy was learning to care a little about other people. "Sleep well."

"Don't let the fleas tickle your knees." He grinned openly for a split second, then turned and walked off to the men's quarters.

She stared after him. He'd never been so plain out nice! Maybe he was growing up. Maybe he appreciated some of the advice she'd offered him often enough.

Her mind clouded, her senses numbed by the

past hectic two days, and she wanted only to flop on the cot and die for a while.

As she slipped out of her boots and unbuckled her belt in the women's quarters, a grand title for a small room with four cots somehow fitting into it, she thought of her man. She always thought of him as that: Her Man. Especially when she was going to bed, whether he was with her or not. Most times he was off gallivanting in some wild place trying to solve somebody else's problem.

When are you going to find time to solve my problem? she thought as she lay down on the cot.

He'd helped her out of a bad hole once, but then he forgot there were other traps along the way, like once was never enough to save a woman.

She'd been down, all right, in Abilene, Kansas, but she hadn't taken up sporting. It wasn't that she wasn't asked.

Her first husband, Rolfe St. Martin, had looked like mighty fine husband material when she met him in Fort Worth.

Her pa had gone off and lost his life in the war, and her mother was ailing so much, she needed a nurse living with them. By then her mother's family had lost everything and moved back to Mexico.

There was never enough money from her wages as a teacher in the grammar school, even though she made a third more than most clerks, and she was gradually selling off the few heirlooms remaining, until she could see that in six months, there would be nothing to sell, no money for a nurse, and no solution.

It was then she prayed her mother wouldn't suffer much longer. Better to die as a human being than as a dog in an alley.

She kept up the appearances so that the old lady never knew how close they were to moving down to the squatters' camp on the river. She never knew anything toward the end except it was all proper and she died a death that didn't disturb her sense of propriety. She never knew how lucky she was to die in her own bed, because it wasn't really her bed anymore. Kate had sold it to a speculator who thought the old lady wouldn't last long. She obliged. Then the school board had fired her for cussin' out loud.

That was when she hit bottom, except along came Rolfe St. Martin, picking up the package she'd dropped in the butcher shop, then escorting her home.

There was nothing holding her in Fort Worth, and Rolfe's impassioned proposal was welcome. She knew she didn't love him, but at twenty years old, she was practically an old maid, and decided she would never love anyone the way they wrote in the romances.

Certainly Rolfe St. Martin was a handsome, well-set-up man with a dark complexion and black hair that was slicked down like patent leather.

He suggested they live in his family home in

Abilene, and like the fool she was, she went with him, only to find he rented a room in a dingy rooming house.

"Never mind, dear love, give me a little time and I'll redeem our home from that rascal of a banker."

He pointed out the family home where the banker lived in high style and explained that if he could only pay the note off in time, he could regain possession.

"I wish I could help," she'd said.

"Maybe you can," he'd said mysteriously.

The next thing she knew, she'd been introduced to the tubby little banker with very fast hands, and had to give him a black eye to prove she meant what she said. She hadn't known that Rolfe had collected in advance on the promise of her body.

Then she learned that he wasn't a property investment counselor, he was a pimp and gambler who had killed three men in the border towns, and had no intention of changing his ways.

"From now on, when I bring a man to your room, you will entertain him just as he likes," Rolfe St. Martin had said, tracing his initial on her breast with a small dagger.

"Wrong," she'd said, and brought her knee up between his legs, and dropped him.

She'd been a tall, dark-haired, pretty girl at the time. After that the effort to stay alive and clean had thinned her down and put small lines in her face.

Then Wayne Carrol had drifted into town and

saw her scrubbing the floors in the Palace Hotel.

She'd worn her hair down over her ears and with a bun at the nape of her neck and wore a gray flannel dress that was ugly enough to discourage even a drunk cowboy that hadn't seen a female in four months.

But veteran Wayne saw through her disguise, saw the young womanhood going to waste and was proud to know her. He didn't treat her like a scrubwoman or a sporter, he just treated her like an old friend that needed to talk some, and after she'd poured out her story, he asked, "You're still married to that skunk?"

She'd nodded miserably and stared at the floor.

"As I see it, solving this problem is easy as eatin' pecan pie." He smiled and patted her shoulder.

"There's no way," she'd said softly. "I'm tied to Rolfe. He won't never let loose of me until I do his bidding."

"It's settled, child," Wayne said, "and you don't even have to marry a man twice your age."

"What?"

"We'll see, sweetheart." And he'd kissed her a little bit, but then she'd kissed him a lot, and that seemed to make things even.

Later that night, Wayne strolled down to the Elephant and played a little three-card monte with the slick-haired St. Martin, and after losing every hand, said, "You're mighty fast with your hands, dealer."

"I can deal slower," St. Martin had replied.

"That'd be some reckless," Wayne said.

"Meanin'?"

"Meanin' you're double-dealin', depending on the bottom card."

He wasn't much for giving the other man a fair chance if he thought he was in the right in the first place, so that when Rolfe St. Martin triggered off the coat-sleeve single-shooter, Wayne had already blown his heart out his back ribs.

St. Martin's big slug came close to earmarking Wayne, but it wouldn't have done St. Martin any good if he'd put it between Wayne's eyes, because he was already as dead as you can get.

Everyone said it was a fair fight, especially the two jaspers named Frank McCloud and Leonardo Fajardo.

There was no one to argue about it. A dead gambler is about as lonesome as a single poker chip, and the whole thing was forgotten before the Friday paper came out announcing the marriage of Katherine St. Martin née Comstock to Wayne D. Carrol.

═══ 4 ═══

SHIG RADIGUET SPURRED THE BUCKSKIN, NOT because the good horse wasn't willing or that they would reach San Luis any sooner, but because he goddamned felt like it. Bletcher, while no better tempered, wasn't as accomplished a rider, and was content to hang on to the saddle horn and let his pinto follow close behind.

With their late start they had to buck the beating sun reflecting back from the alkali, which made Shig Radiguet all the more dangerous.

He felt as if he'd already been rawhided enough by that sweet-talkin' split-tail without havin' to be roasted alive out in the white-rimmed desert, especially when he didn't think they'd gone south anyways.

Crossin' the border seemed like a good idea if you wanted to hide out because the damned greasers'd gang up on a gringo lawman, but there was nothing down this way except some mop-haired Indians eating chuckwallas and grasshoppers, and Wayne Carrol had a reputation for associating with a higher type of people.

Still it had to be checked out. It would be just like the old fox to lay a double trail, so you think he's goin' to San Luis but you're dead sure he's going somewhere else, while all the time he's really settin' in the shade in San Luis drinking beer.

Wasn't far. Course, he could just cross anywhere, but San Luis was the only waterin' hole for miles either way, and Shig Radiguet didn't think the old fox was capable of just living off sand and alkali.

The pair passed an old man riding a burro, his bare toes dragging the sand, and in an hour came into the haphazardly organized village which consisted mainly of scattered flat-roofed, colorless, dusty adobes and trash piles smoldering in the heat.

There was a Mexican border official living there somewhere, but no one paid him any attention. His home and office was just another featureless adobe with the exception of a fairly straight mesquite flagpole planted in front. There was no flag, the last having been chewed to rags by the hungry sun, and it wasn't thought worthwhile to keep feeding flags to that visitor who never left for very long.

The only place of importance was the two-story Cantina de las Rosas, which had no doors because it never closed. In the back of the bar were a couple of rooms for the proprietor's family. Upstairs were a couple of rooms for the *putas*, a pair of short-legged masa balls with hair starting low on their foreheads who sat and waited most of the day and night.

Shig Radiguet left his frothed buckskin out in the sun and strode into the dark cantina that seemed to be a little cooler than the pure hades outside.

He glanced at the whores, like fat lumps of mud at a corner table, and went to the bar, where he rapped on it with a silver dime.

The proprietor, a small, enterprising, middle-aged man, came in from the family rooms in the back and said, "Yes, *señor*," as Bletcher came straggling in.

"Beer, is it cold?"

"Cold? Yes, indeed, of course, it's so cold it will make your teeth ache."

Putting two glasses of warm beer on the bar, he took the dime and started to leave, when Radiguet snarled, "Just a damned minute, stupid, I want some answers."

"Sí, señor."

"I'm looking for a skinny old fart with a gray mustache, riding a chestnut gelding probably. Maybe has a dark, good-looking woman with him and a smart-ass kid."

"No, they haven't crossed here." The proprietor shrugged his shoulders.

"How do you know?" Bletcher put in meanly.

"Everyone stops here, coming and going." The proprietor stepped back from the bar as he saw the anger boiling in these powerful gringos.

"Are you sure?" Shig Radiguet snarled. "Did they pay you to lie?"

"You can't trust the sons a bitches," Bletcher said, eyeing the sweating Mexican like a lynx watching a fat quail.

"Oh, that man with the gray mustache?" the Mexican exclaimed as if remembering. "Somebody said he was going on down to Sonoita. Maybe he's down there."

"He'd say anything to get us out of here," Shig Radiguet said to Bletcher.

"I can sweat the truth out of him in less'n a minute," Bletcher muttered.

"We got to figure what's in Carrol's mind. How was he thinking last night? What did he want? Was the split-tail in on it?"

"He'd be thinkin' about the payroll money."

"Maybe. But he was moanin' about cached treasure just before he passed out in the hotbox."

"I never heard anybody say anything about a treasure in these parts." Bletcher shook his blocky head.

"That's it! There ain't nothing within a hundred miles of Fort Yuma. Nothin' but worthless Injuns who don't know what a gold nugget looks like."

"So?" Bletcher asked.

"So he's gone east."

"Why east?"

"There's no treasure west or north, or south. There ain't nothing but stinkin' greasers like this fat, lying son of a bitch."

"There ain't a hell of a lot of anything east either."

"We're wastin' time."

Shig Radiguet gulped down the rest of his warm beer and strode across the packed earth floor, kicked a sleeping pig in the butt, and climbed aboard the sweat-stained buckskin.

"Back to Fort Yuma. We'll change horses and travel."

"Can't we take a stage?" Bletcher groaned, climbing up on the pinto.

"I travel light and fast." Shig Radiguet grinned, showing his broken tooth. "And I get there first."

Kate stretched out lazily on the cot and snuggled the pillow to her face, having a sweet dream that Wayne was beside her, holding her head on his furry brisket in a troubleless world.

A troublesome sunbeam touched her closed eyes and she tried to hold on to the tranquil dream, but the coming of the day couldn't be held back, and she awakened with a groan of protest.

Why couldn't life be like that, just drifting along pleasantly, never a crisis, never a worry, just go on with your family without a care in the world?

It's not that way, girl, she told herself. Too bad, but nobody rich or poor gets to live like that.

She sat on the edge of the cot and put her face in her hands, her elbows on her knees, thinking of some way to keep the dream alive or make it possible at least, but there was no way so long as Wayne kept rambling around like the Darby ram.

She smelled coffee brewing in the other room and washed her face in a big china basin, brushed her hair, tied it back with a ribbon, and went into the dining room.

She was pleased that she'd awakened before Tyson. She said good morning to the cook and poured herself a cup of coffee.

They could be at Red Butte Station in half a day with the horses grained and rested.

The coffee finished, she became uneasy, and crossed the yard to the men's quarters. An old

Mexican was sweeping a few puffs of lint and dust out the front door.

"Would you please wake up the young man," she asked.

"Who?" the sweeper asked, confused as if the problem were overwhelming.

"The young man with the head of reddish hair." She smiled.

"Ain't nobody in there," the sweeper protested, as if he'd be accused of stealing a tenant. "Look for yourself!"

"No problem," she said, trying to calm the old man down, and looked in the doorway.

There were six cots, all made up with gray blankets and all empty.

Just like his dad! she thought instantly, angry at the whole tribe of Carrol men who felt they could just up and run whether anyone else had an objection or not.

Stalking back to the dining room, she asked the cook if she'd seen the boy leave.

"No, ma'am. I was up at about four and nobody left."

So he probably never went to bed. He lied to her like a possum in a corn patch, smilin' away all peachy cream pie, taking her for a goddamned greenhorn *pendeja*!

Once mounted with a full canteen of water and a package of cornbread and fried sowbelly in her pack, she rode the bay out on the trail.

Reining in suddenly, she thought, right now I can change my life. I can go down the trail to Red Butte where those goddamned lying, cheating Carrols might be, or I can go west to California and find me a rich gold miner.

My gold miner will build me a mansion on Nob Hill and pile up gold and diamonds in my hope chest. He'll send to China for the best silks, and he'll bring in a seamstress from France to make my dresses. The floors will be marble, and maybe even the walls. . . . We'll take a steamboat to England and meet the queen.

Now's the time to make up your mind, girl; you'll be havin' a birthday next month, and I reckon your gold miner is going to have eyes for a younger bird right soon.

What gold miner? she asked herself suddenly, and laughed at her imagination.

"C'mon, bay horse, my man's goin' to need help whether he knows it or not."

She kneed the bay down the trail southeast, feeling easier in her mind. She'd show those Carrol men just what a good, clean-cut cowgirl could do on her own. Next time she wouldn't believe a word either one of 'em said, and if there were lies to be told, she'd be doing the tellin'.

She knew she could make better time in the daylight than Tyson could last night in the darkness. She weighed about the same as he did, and her horse was stronger for having the rest and the grain, so she kicked him into a slow gallop that was as sweet as a rockin' chair. The bay could rest when they came to Red Butte Station.

She paid little attention to the spiny verdure growing on either side of the trail. Once in a while she'd surprise a deer or an antelope, but there was no one out traveling that early in the morning.

Later on she met a freight wagon drawn by four straining mules, but she just waved and was gone before the driver could spit and say howdy.

Going downhill over the well-made trail, she made good time. It was even cooler in the tree country where the piñons and oaks soaked up the sun, and the high air seemed to just let it pass on through.

She let the big bay keep his best pace, doing what he liked most, his big shoulders rocking and his hindquarters making the long stride effortlessly, hardly feeling her weight as an impediment.

Still, as they came into the lower country, drier and rockier, the heat increased and the sun overhead commenced taking its toll on the good horse.

His breath was deep and more hoarse, and he was working harder to maintain his stride, and sweat soaked his dark hide.

She had no idea of how long she'd ridden or how far. There were no signboards and she had no watch. Judging from the bay's hoarse breathing, they had been on the slow gallop long enough, and it was all that she should ask this day of the willing horse.

"We've got to be close," she said aloud, hoping to encourage the horse. "Give me another half hour if you can."

She tried to sit her saddle better, leaning forward and keeping her legs close to his heaving barrel, trying to make it as easy as possible for him.

He carried on, until they reached the level plateau where the trail followed a dry wash across hard volcanic country and sharp red rocks littered the trail.

"Can't do it," she said, and reined the bay down to a slow trot. Sweat streamed off his chocolate reddish hide, but he held his head high as if he were pleased to go out for a morning's breeze.

Riding a regular wagon road with the moon to light his path, young Tyson Carrol had little trouble finding the way. True enough, he couldn't hurry it, because there could be any kind of a hazard on the trail, but he could go at a fast trot that, though his backbone and butt took a beating, still made good time, and kept him awake.

He had a guilty conscience about leaving Kate at the station, but she'd made it so there could be no other way. If he'd told the truth, she'd have insisted on going with him, or even going on ahead of him as if she could protect him from a danger she didn't even know about.

No, if she'd just settle down and keep out of a man's business, so you could count on her to fry bacon and flapjacks for breakfast, sweep the floor, gather the eggs, and wash the blankets once in a while, that'd be useful, but with her of a mind to get into the middle of his own personal plans, what could you do with her?

Mainly he wanted to find his dad before his dad got himself into a briar patch of trouble.

It wasn't so much that the old man went out huntin' trouble all the time. Sometimes, yes, he did, but most times he just would be ridin' along and he'd find himself inside a whirlwind where some poor soul would be beggin' for money he didn't have and couldn't get honestly. With so much experience, you'd think he'd learn to never leave the front porch.

Like there he was in Abilene instead of cuttin' hay on the rented place they had over on the Blue River near Vermillion. What the hell was he doing in Abilene?

The dumb rooster was struttin' high in deep mud getting himself married. Hardly knew the girl, and she was half his age, and could just as well have been a sister, but no, he falls for a hard-luck story, downs the coyote husband, but that ain't enough, he's got to turn around and make it legal.

Tyson didn't know anything about her except what he saw when his dad brought her to the farm and left her after a couple days without sayin' where he was going or how long he'd be away.

"It's his way," Tyson had said, and went back to haying.

Kate had started walking the floor back and forth.

"He's in trouble, I know it," she said that night.

"Likely," Tyson had agreed. "That's what he does most."

He knew enough about places like Abilene and the women that lived off the cowboys to know that the woman sat on an ace of spades and it took some money to get her to show it. At least that's what he'd heard cowboys sobering up say, not that he knew much about it, at the age of fifteen, but being close to the animals, he couldn't very well not know nothing about it.

He'd heard sporters could make a deal of money with their hide-out ace of spades, take a peggin' every five minutes, but then they never figured on the future and threw it all away on something worthless.

That's what the old men settin' on the bench in front of the mercantile said, like as if they knew what they was talkin' about. He could understand his pa renting the use of the ace for five minutes, but why did he have to buy the whole deck?

And he wouldn't say nothin' to explain it.

Ride in all red and short a breath, and say, this here's your new stepmom, Kate. You two can get acquainted while I ride off towards Peru or Argentina, someplace you could never get back from.

After a day and a night, she asked him, "He does this regular?"

"Yes, ma'am. He does."

"Don't change?"

"Ma, nor me, nor folks you'd call close ever could change him."

"So you just wait until he feels damned good and ready to come back and say hello."

"That's so, ma'am."

"Call me Kate, Tyson," she said. "Seems like we're goin' to be close enough to use the same toothpick."

"Reckon I better get that hay raked and stacked before it rains," Tyson had said, and skedaddled faster'n a turped cat. Women, decent or not, were critters to keep across a couple rivers.

She cooked him a full-sized breakfast next morning, and before he could run off, she sat across the table and asked, "Where is he?"

"Can't say."

"Do you know?"

"No, ma'am. He couldn't be more'n two days' ride from the Blue River, though."

"I'm a little slow," she said, "but I have a feeling you can tell me he's with two other gents. Yes or no."

"Likely. I couldn't say for sure." He'd lied for the first time. Or at least he hadn't come out and flatshat told her what he thought, which was it was ninety-nine to one that his dad was riding right

65

now with Frank and Leonardo, figuring to make the big stake that would give them peace and security forevermore.

"Frank and Leonardo," she said, "that scant yellow-haired one wider than a grizzly's gut and the Mexican who couldn't see over a swayback burro?"

"That'd be them," Tyson had agreed.

"And what're they doin'?"

"I never ask what they're doin', and they don't say," Tyson said, rising from the table. "You don't happen to have a kid sister, do you?" he blurted out because it had been on his mind all night.

"Me?" Then she softened. "No, Tyson; I sure as hell wish I did, though."

"Just wonderin'," Tyson said, plunging out the door and running toward the hayfield like as if the green would turn brown if he didn't get there soon enough.

Later in the morning she brought him down a jar of lemonade and some cinnamon rolls. They sat off to one side under a black walnut and she said, "I been thinkin' this through."

"Yes'm, Kate."

"They went somewhere to stick up a bank, you think?"

"It ain't mine to fret," he answered miserably. "Best not say more. It ain't our business."

"The hell it ain't!" she howled. "Ain't your life your business? Ain't mine, mine?"

"But his is his'n."

"No, there's the kicker. When you get married by law, you lose that. You give it away. He don't have his'n no more, he has our'n."

"Yes'm, Kate."

"That means you got to tell me where they went."

"I'd guess they went west."

"How far west?"

"Can't go too far. They's an ocean they say cuts you off."

"Damn it, Tyson. Be serious. What does this piece of paper mean to you?" she demanded, bringing out a kind of a map written on the back of a paper bag.

"There's an X here where it says Blue. There's an X where it says Abilene. Then on yonder is an X where it says Tres Cruces."

"Don't ask me."

"I am asking you."

"Ma'am, Kate, stay out of it."

"They're goin' to rob a bank or something in Tres Cruces," she decided. "I've got to stop him before he gets in trouble."

"He's always either in trouble or just gettin' out," Tyson said, afraid she just might make a run for it with the bit in her teeth.

"Three of them. What's there in Tres Cruces?"

"It's just a stage station and little town."

"We've got to stop them," Kate said. "Suppose they get caught?"

"Suppose they come out with a sackful of

hundred-dollar gold pieces?" he asked.

"You said there was nothing there, and that includes money," she said firmly.

"They're gone. We can't catch 'em. We wait."

"No, Tyson, no no. There's the telegraph nowadays. I could send him a wire easy enough."

"To where?"

"Tres Cruces."

"Oh hell, don't meddle, ma'am, Kate."

"Don't you want to save your dad from prison or bein' shot down like a yeller dog?"

"He always told me never interfere with nothin' that ain't botherin' you none."

"But I'm his wife. I've got a right."

"I doubt he figured that in the bargain."

"What bargain?"

Tyson flushed a bright red, and decided he'd said too much.

"What bargain?" she insisted.

"Whatever it costs to buy the ace of spades." Tyson's voice came out husky and broken.

"What the hell are you talking about, Tyson Carrol!" Kate shrieked in frustration, her mind hating to admit that the boy was born a loony.

After a long period of silence while each tried to figure out what the other was talking about, Kate had stood up, run her hands through her long black hair, and said, "I'm going to do it."

"Don't. He'll be back," Tyson had said, shaking his head.

"You're too young to understand," she said.

"I been ridin' in the back of this wagon quite a spell, ma'am, and I'm gettin' a belly full of it too."

"We both need him too much to lose him," she said, and rode her pony clear over to Marysville, where there was a telegraph office, and sent the message blind:

Mr. Wayne Carrol
c/o Western Union
Tres Cruces, New Mexico
DON'T DO IT. COME HOME. KATE.

That's a pretty good joke, the telegrapher thought, taking her money, but he didn't go on to explain that every telegrapher west of the Mississippi knew that name. Less than a year before a man name of Wayne Carrol had stuck up the Western Union in Creede, Colorado, and got away slick as a cat's ass.

Funny she didn't know. That's why it must be a joke of some kind, he thought, appaising her full figure under the cover of his green eyeshade.

He wanted to ask what she thought Wayne Carrol was going to do, but looking at her set jaw and wide spaced, dark eyes, thought better of it. Get yourself slapped down sniffin' around that stuff.

For her part, Kate couldn't figure why the telegrapher was grinning. "Will it be there by tomorrow?"

"Oh yes, I'll put a rush order on it." The telegrapher chuckled.

Drunk or crazy, she thought. Anyway I did my best.

═══ 5 ═══

ANTS HAD DISCOVERED THE SLUMPED FORM of Wayne Carrol where he lay half-in, half-out of the sun in the jumble of red rocks.

Their scouts tentatively mapped the enormous project ahead of them, and their engineers worked out the quickest way to haul the massive meal below ground before the buzzards and coyotes came along.

Workers were called from far and wide and organized into meat brigades, while others expanded the warehouses under the baked earth to accommodate the huge windfall.

Unfortunately for the ants, one of the scouts took a bite out of the scarred forearm of the downed outlaw which sent a message running into his mental survival center that said: Ants!

Another stinging nip on the leg, and another on the back of the neck, tripled the emphasis on this message, and the disorganized man began to coordinate; cables were repaired, nerve ends grafted, pools of memory oxygenated, the stagnant blood booted in the butt, as the pumps caught the crisis signal.

Blindly and unthinking he brushed at the sore spots, and rolled half over, which ruined the ants' entire plan, making it necessary to estimate the job all over again.

Higher authority sent down word that before you can haul it away, you must first kill it. To do that took a thousand ants, each with its minute load of poison, which, if the work went properly, should first paralyze the great lump of protein and ultimately kill it from shock.

The killer brigades hardly got started before the hulk rolled away, and lifted itself so that it leaned on its two arms, its head hanging down.

It was about this time that a sparked thought crossed through the darkness: move.

And yet the thought fizzled into a pool that by its dead weight said: no.

Another flare in the darkness said: move!

And this time, another followed: now!

He groaned. The ache sledging inside his head was enough to make him retch, and he couldn't bear to open his eyes.

Feeling the ant bites, he began brushing his clothes frantically without looking.

But then it came to the point the ant stings were hurting more than the bass drum inside his head, and he had to open his eyes to see what the problem was.

The problem was the anthill a few feet away from him. He rolled again and half climbed a rock, then brushed off more of the persistent critters who hated to lose the dream of devouring so much so close to home.

"Cut it out, you sons a bitches!" he yelled, his eyes closed again.

Batting at his legs, he staggered farther away and collapsed in the shade of a tilted slab of rock.

A sidewinder buzzed from the dark angle and he instinctively backed off and found another spot of shade.

"What what what?" the high command demanded of the lower echelons, but all the replies were the same: I didn't do it.

"I did it!" he yelled again. "I turned my back on a goddamned missionary!"

"Son of a bitch!" He groaned softly so as to not short any more circuits.

"Easy, Wayne," he whispered, "don't get violent. Give yourself a chance. Take your time; it'll be all right in a week or so if you don't push too hard. No good bustin' a gut just from bein' mad."

Where the hell are you, old-timer?

His energy rose and fell, memory failing, then restored, then drifting off again.

Hell of a knock on the *cabeza*, Wayne.

It wasn't the missionary, it was his woman.

My horse?

That's it. They needed the horse. They wouldn't walk.

Pieces of the scene popped into his mind and

fell off to one side, slowly making a reconstruction that he could study on.

He opened his eyes again, but he could see only the vaguest forms in front of him. He tried to look at his hand, but it was only a shimmer of color lighter than the background.

Knocked your eyes out, he thought despite the throbbing that seemed to intensify whenever he tried to think.

How we goin' to do this?

Do what?

Get someplace.

Where?

Water. Cool. Time.

Jesus, my head!

"Cowboys don't moan," he said out loud, firming up his jaw, which had shown a tremor of sad resignation. "Take your time, buckaroo, no hurry."

Nobody's waitin'. The poignant thought passed by unnoticed except that it served to keep a connection with the living.

With the horse went the canteen, he thought as he felt his lips cracking, and his mouth too dry to make spit.

Soon's you git your head spliced on again, you goin' to go it the hard way.

I dunno—he sank back—I dunno. You might make a mile or two, but you can't even start off without eyes.

It'll clear up, another sector of the apparatus responded.

Where was I? Damn. Where was I? Out in the *mala país*. Yes. Remember that, but why?

Looking for somethin'? The cache?

What cache?

Dunno. He shook his head and opened his eyes again, forcing his eyelids to hold up until, despite his willing otherwise, they dropped and closed.

Shortcut. That's it. Cuttin' off the bight. Why?

Save time.

Where?

How the hell do I know? Texas. Wyoming. Nevada. Idaho.

Nevada. Arizona.

Yuma! All right!

As the time passed, his thoughts became more rational and positive.

He remembered Yuma. Place to stay away from. He remembered Shig Radiguet, the warden, and the guard named Puto Bletcher.

But they were somewhere back yonder, somewhere in a painful haze. They were not threats, they were only pasteboard cutouts of a torture sometime in the past. Compared to the pain in his head, the stinging ant bites, the dryness paining his whole body, they were in a different world.

Then the picture of the red butte flipped through his mind and he had the proper clue.

Hell, it's only ten miles maybe. No more'n twenty. Can't go it if you can't see it.

He opened his eyes again and stood up. Turning a slow circle, he tried to see a picture that would match his memory of the red butte rising over a great expanse of brown earth.

Nothing. Just the shimmering light and dark.

Slumping down again, he tried to keep calm. Without eyes, he was a goner. Even with sight, it was nigh on impossible to walk that far in this kind of country in this kind of heat.

Damn it, he had something to do. Something important!

What?

What the hell difference does it make!

Well, old-timer, you seen some country and rode some trails nobody ever knew.

C'mon, damn it, eyes, see something! he commanded angrily from his despair. He had something important that had to be done before he cashed in. Cache. What the hell was he thinking about? What had he cached?

He lifted the unwilling eyelid of his right eye and looked at his left hand. He didn't see the hand, but he saw a shape. Well, that's an improvement.

For damned sure something is better'n nothin'.

Just tell me where the sun is, eyes, and we'll be on our way.

He figured it must be afternoon by now and if he could just be sure the sun was on his back, he'd come out on the plain, close to Red Butte Station. Someone would see him if he could just get out on the flats.

What he didn't reckon was that it was early morning when he'd encountered the Nariz prophesiers, and that he'd been unconscious about an hour, which put the time at a little before ten in the morning.

Gradually his vision improved until he could make out genuine shadows and infer from their direction that they were pointing east.

In that he was dead wrong. The sun was not westerly, it was still morning and the sun was still in the east.

That's it, he thought, just follow the shadows of the rocks and you'd be in there in a couple hours or so.

Couldn't just lie around out here and get cooked. Need water pretty bad. Can't think on it.

Groaning and staggering on rubbery legs, he grimly made the decision, and headed the wrong way.

Couple hours, we'll hit the flats. People can see ten miles across there, it's so clear. Likely some good man will come out to help, he thought, trying to get into the proper frame of mind for a hellish walk.

His boots were too small, as befitted a man who didn't walk, and the heels were high for fitting stirrups, or plowing the ground in bulldogging a thousand-pound longhorn.

Don't fret about it. You ain't got any choice, less'n a couple missionaries come along you can hit in the head with a rock. He grinned, and then shuddered from the pain of making a joke.

As the shadows slowly shortened, he began to wonder.

Can't be. Just can't be. Too much sun. Not enough water. You ain't seeing clear.

Yet while he knew the westering sun would make the shadows lengthen, they definitely were disappearing as if the sun were approaching noon directly overhead.

Oh God, he thought suddenly, I did it this time.

Couldn't be any other way. He'd gone west toward the Gila fifty miles away instead of east toward the red butte.

Guessed it wrong, Wayne, and now you goin' to pay the hard way.

You done burned yourself out goin' backwards, he thought, and even as he realized his vision was improving, his strength was running out.

Got to backtrack all that way, he accused himself. Got to do it.

Why? Why not take a rest in the shade and try it in the night maybe? The thought passed through his torpid brain and he recognized it as the first sign of approaching death.

He knew it well enough from past times. Your brain starts saying it's so nice to just lie down and take it easy while each part of you slowly gives itself up, until it's so damned comfortable, you're nodding off, and you don't never wake up.

C'mon, Wayne, you old devil, get your feet to movin'.

Turning dreamily, he knew there were no shadows with the sun overhead and no directions. He ought to wait a while, but if he stopped, he just doubted if he could ever get started again.

He wasn't sweating any, his carcass was so dried out, but the blisters on his feet were seeping painfully.

He could make out his own boot tracks, and he'd been in such bad shape, he hadn't covered all that much ground in the morning. Maybe he could follow his own tracks back. If he lost them, then he'd have to stop for sure.

His vision was almost normal close up, and he could see the boot scrapes in sand pockets between the chocolate-colored rocks, as he painfully retraced his trail.

He was at least going in the right direction, and in an hour of dull, painful trudging, his eyes had cleared enough that he thought he could make out the red butte rising up out of a silver shimmering lake.

"That's all right, eyes," he said out loud, "I don't mind you showing me a mirage, just don't lose track of that butte."

His mind seemed to separate from his body as he limped along through the *mala país*, the butte appearing no closer, serving only as a monument to the faint hope of survival still hanging on in his breast.

He wanted to sing something, and thought about it, something to cheer him up or signify that his life had amounted to something in its time and place:

I'll eat when I'm hungry, I'll drink when I'm dry,
If the hard times don't kill me, I'll live till I die. . . .
Rye whiskey, rye whiskey, rye whiskey, I cry,
If you don't give me rye whiskey, I sholly will die. . . .

Wasn't much there, he thought grimly, shaking his head. He hadn't been that much of a boozer. He'd hung around with a lot of them, but more to take care of them when they went crazy.

No, he wasn't so much of a wild one, not a woman's man, neither. Seemed like he was always just a little outside the gang. No one wanted to fight him, but they couldn't just all nest together very long either because he'd get to feelin' restless, and they knew he was a rambler, so there wasn't much sense in going out of the way to do him any big, long-lasting favors.

"Fine with me, buckaroos," he said aloud. "Just let me wear my own boots and ride my own horse."

I never did any harm to a decent man that I know of. Them I killed wasn't decent—they was banking people, law bullies, bounty hunters, bossy types. That ain't America, the land of the free and home of the brave.

Anybody buckin' my country's founding fathers can't be called decent, and if they put their weight against me, then I just stand on my rights and take hold the old Colt and make some changes. George Washington give us guns to get rid of the bossy types.

Course, a grasshopper don't carry much baggage even if he covers a lot of ground. God, I was a fool kid when I jumped out of Pittsburg and headed for Chicago. Kind of like Tyson, but not so serious. Wasn't a railroad west of the Big River. Wasn't nothing but grass up to a tall horse's belly, and green as emeralds.

Million buffaloes over there, feeding the Indians, making 'em tepees and robes.

Antelope jumping around like fleas on a old dog, and deer and wild horses, so pretty you could almost cut out a piece of it and hang it in a frame on the wall. But it was one of a piece; every time you cut a piece of it out, it died all the more.

A million pigeons, a million ducks and geese, a million beavers and foxes and bears. A million cat-fish, a million trout, and more'n a million salmon coming up the western rivers every spring.

What'd you do with it, buckaroo?

Nothin'. Rode over it. Fed myself and my horse, but I never fenced it nor changed the water, nor did nothing to make my bed any softer. All I did was ride over it and look at it so's I would always remember the big pasture sloping up to the Rockies, and the parks of Colorado, and the Missouri breaks and the badlands on west. I just wanted to see it all and come to an understanding with it same as when I used to watch the stars turn overhead ridin' nighthawk on a herd, or same as hearing a mountain stream tumbling down all night making such a pretty music that never stopped. It went on day and night and maybe still is, just singing away with all the joy freedom gives.

I was looking, all right, to shame the devil and tell the truth, I was looking for the high valley with the stream down the middle and up and down mountains all around it to keep off the big snows, and hold some sun. Sure I was looking and seen a few too, but they was always somebody coming along had a bigger need than me, and so I traveled on like a sugar-footed loner, playing the fool most times.

But then the Cache. No, they ain't nothin' like that nowhere else. By God, I don't mean to take it and make it suit my comforts, but I aim to take it because I saw it first and I deserve it most.

Can't do it alone.

Frank and Leonardo? Can ask.

Got a chance with Tyson if he'll ever quit fightin' folks and a chance with Kate if she'll stick to her own knittin'. . . .

It's lions. It's lions that make the cache. It ain't coyote country at all. It's for lions and eagles and horses to match and men to hold it.

Oh, how them mountains punch into the sky! Snow just so cold and clear in the shade of green pine trees sending out the water, the cold splashing water, singing over the cobblestones in the creek bed, all day and all night, never stoppin'. Say, that's the song for me. . . .

Wayne staggered and fell. A buzzard altered the angle of his spread wings and slipped off his thermal to take a whiff of what looked like a promising dinner.

The dun mare gave Tyson all she could until he saw the squat ranch buildings at the base of the butte. A few mesquite trees grew on the plain, but the grass had already been burned down by the summer's heat, and absence of rain.

He could see the ranch buildings and a corral of horses even though he was still miles away. The air was so clear, he could have made out a walking man, if there'd been one.

No hurry now, no need to ride in with a foam-slopped horse. Walk her in, let her cool down some.

Nobody could ride in or out of that station without him seeing them.

As he came closer, Tyson looked for the distinctive chestnut gelding in the corral, but it was just a bunch of paint mustangs someone was breaking for riding stock.

Too early or too late, he thought, not worrying it just yet.

There was another corral where relay stage teams could be caught and harnessed in a hurry, but there was no chestnut in there either.

He tethered the dun under a pepper tree near the front of the double log cabin with a covered dog run between, and called, "Hello the house."

An old man wearing gray trousers, red suspenders, and no shirt came to the entrance, peered out, and called back, "Come on in out of the sun."

A fresh breeze passed through the shaded dog run, and as Tyson came in out of the sun, he wondered if this geezer was like all the rest of the old top doggers.

"Set down, son. It's time for dinner."

"Already?" Tyson had lost track of the time. If it was noontime already, his dad should have been here hours before.

"I'm looking for a feller on a chestnut gelding. Got a gray mustache and stands tall."

"Nobody like that in here today. Fact is," the old man cackled, "you're the first one in since the missionaries stopped by yesterday. I figured they'd be back soon enough, but maybe they made it on across the *mala país*."

"Missionaries?" Tyson asked.

"Man and a woman. Wouldn't believe me. Had God on their side, they said. Not too likable."

"Speakin' of the devil"—the old man sighted over the plain—"that sure looks like your chestnut and my missionaries all in one parcel."

Tyson went to the doorway and looked across the heat-shimmering plain. The old man's eyes were better trained for seeing across the distance, but he could make out a horse carrying two people slowly from the west.

"Woman," the old man yelled into the house, "got a couple more to feed pretty soon."

"It ain't right." Tyson let out his breath slowly. "That chestnut is my pa's favorite horse; he'll be branded with our Circle C."

"Maybe he got set afoot out there, maybe he died," the old man said. "Lots of damfools do."

"My pa ain't no damfool." Tyson glared at the old man. "They's something wrong. When they stop in here, you better keep that horse."

"Why should I interfere in somebody else's business?" The old man frowned.

" 'Cause they stoled that horse, and I mean to see 'em hang for it, and I'd hate to know you was mixed up with horse thieves," Tyson said bleakly, staring at the old man, and moving closer.

"Sure, boy, anything you say," the old man muttered, looking at the floor. "That horse will be finished for a day at least anyways. And likely them two are, too."

Tyson mounted the dun, and rode at an easy gallop across the barren plain to intercept the jaded chestnut.

The woman, riding behind the saddle, had a switch made from a mesquite branch and was whipping the horse on either flank, but the chestnut could go no faster.

"The Prophet of Nariz be praised," the man in the shiny suit cried out as Tyson approached.

"Get down off that horse," Tyson said. "Can't you see he's finished?"

"That's a strange way to greet a messenger of the Lord," the man said, his hand slowly moving toward the gun belt hanging from the saddle horn.

"Mister, you make the eenciest wrong move, I'm going to kill you deader'n hell. Where's my pa?"

"We don't know your pa," the woman said.

Tyson palmed his ancient six-shooter, rode the dun directly at the pair, and clubbed the man on the shoulder.

"I said get down off that horse."

"Fine, fine," the man whimpered, slipping out of the stirrups.

"You'll answer for this!" the woman stormed.

"Get down."

"You dumb kid, get out of my way!"

The woman's face contorted with vicious hatred

as she suddenly lashed Tyson across the face with the mesquite switch.

The resulting explosion and bloom of black powder smoke seemed all the greater in the empty barrens.

Through watering, painful eyes, Tyson saw the hat disappear in fragments of red cherries and black-dyed straw, and a fine red wet line appeared exactly in the part of the woman's hair.

She dropped the switch, closed her eyes, and slipped off the horse in a dead faint, blood running down her face.

Tyson looked at the old .45 with amazement.

"Somebody filed the sear down and made it a hair trigger. . . ." he said, as if explaining the event to himself, "and she shoots a hair lower'n I figured too."

"She's bleeding to death!" the man cried out, wiping the trickle of blood off her face.

"No." Tyson looked down at the woman. "Those scalp wounds always look a lot worse'n they are."

"You've murdered a bride of Nariz!" the man moaned.

Suddenly Tyson felt the power of the gun. The equalizer. He'd drawn blood and it felt good. No longer would anyone try to treat him like a child, or try to dominate him. No, not so long as he had the gun would anyone humble him again.

Not Shig Radiguet, or the fat guard Bletcher, or his father, Wayne Carrol.

"Mister, tell me what you did with my pa."

The paunchy man in the black suit looked fearfully at his wife on the ground, and then said, "I don't know anything."

"You want me to take you back out there?" Tyson said, shaking out his lasso and building a loop.

"No, oh, no. No more of that. It's the Lord's miracle that we've survived."

"You killed him?"

"No. He said, being as we were doing God's work, we could ride the horse and he'd walk."

"You lying bastard," Tyson said. "When you get over there to the station, you just have yourself a good rest."

Taking the reins of the chestnut, he left the pair and led the tired horse back to the station.

"It's them, all right. I'd be much obliged if you'd loan me a fresh horse," Tyson said stiffly to the old man.

"You mean your pa is out there in the *mala país*?"

"Them Christians set him afoot." Tyson nodded.

"Help yourself," the old man said sympathetically. "Take the piebald; he's the best for ridin' the rocks. Take the black with the blaze for your pa. Go ahead, get a move on, boy; a man can't live a day out there."

"Yes, sir. I'm beholden to you." Tyson wanted to say he was sorry for being so snorty earlier, but he didn't have the words.

Quickly he caught the two horses, rigged them, and, leading the black, galloped west across the long plain.

When he passed the pair limping along, he didn't bother to touch his hat.

He covered the five miles to the rising red rocks in half an hour, and then let the piebald pick his way through rocks westerly, always keeping an eye on the back trail of the missionary couple.

It must have been about two hours after high noon that Tyson saw the figure, more like a wind-blown scarecrow than a human, staggering through the barren traverses and breaks.

He was talking and singing, falling down, getting up, sometimes feeling his way with his hands.

"Dad," Tyson called, "Dad, just stay there."

He angled the horses over to where old Wayne leaned against a tall red rock, a kind of a smile on his cracked lips.

"Where you been, boy?"

"Nowhere," Tyson said, coming off the piebald with the canteen in his hand. "You?"

"Thinking about the cache, Tyson," Wayne muttered thickly. "When you goin' to grow up?"

"How much more you want?" Tyson asked, putting the canteen to the swollen split lips.

"Not much," old Wayne said, his red-rimmed cat eyes focusing on Tyson's for a second.

6

KATE CAME RIDING DOWN INTO THE LONG plain just as a small wagon train passed her going west.

She noticed a man in a shiny black suit resting in the back of a wagon and a woman alongside of him, her head wrapped in a turban of white bandages.

A young man and his bride sat in front driving the horses. They appeared to be happily in love, pleased to share their goods with someone less fortunate.

The man in back was stuffing his mouth with cornbread and washing it down with a pitcher of milk.

The woman was staring off at the red *mala país*, speaking loudly to the man. "I'll have the law on him! I'll see him hang!"

Kate rode on to the way station at the foot of the butte, and saw the dun and the chestnut in a separate corral eating from grain boxes.

They're here, she thought.

Tethering her bay under the pepper tree, she found the old man with the red suspenders over his bare, sagging shoulders sitting in a split willow chair in the dog run.

"Come set, ma'am," he said, not getting up. "I'm plumb wore out from travelers and one danged thing after another, but you're welcome and you just make yourself to home."

"Thank you."

"Woman," he hollered off into the house, "set another plate."

"I need more wood," came a woman's complaint.

The old man put his finger to his lips and smiled. "She's always sayin' that."

"I see the chestnut and the dun in the corral," Kate said directly.

"Yes'm. You mixed up in this too?"

"Depends," she said, deciding to let somebody else lead the do-si-do for a change.

"They ain't back yet," the old man said. "They got to make it before dark. Ain't no man can live out there all day without water."

"Yonder?" She nodded her head at the rising breaks of red rocks.

"Yes'm. The boy went out on fresh horses, but it ain't easy findin' a downed man out there. I tried it a few times."

"I don't understand."

"Me neither, to tell the truth, but one way or another, a couple of missionaries got ahold of that chestnut and rode in on it. The boy, he cut 'em off and had a powwow, then I guess he didn't get the right answer, so he hauled out his old hog's leg, and to my reckoning, it went off accidental. I can't believe a boy that age, salty as he is, would just mean to shoot that unarmed woman."

"He is some salty." Kate nodded.

"So he took fresh horses and rode off into the rocks."

"How long ago?"

"Two, three hours."

"That's not so long."

"No, but they've got to get out of that hell-trap before dark. It ain't no place to be at night."

"Where's your woodpile?" Kate asked.

"Woodpile?" The old man sounded surprised.

"Your woman needs wood, and I'm able," Kate said, getting to her feet.

"But the men in the *mala país*?"

"They'll either come in or they won't," Kate said, thinking the old bastard would sit on his hind end all day gossiping just so his old woman would be worn out every night.

How do they get that way? What has that old man got that he can make a good woman into his personal slave? she wondered.

It ain't balls, 'cause he's over the hill. It's just somethin' in men that makes them arrogant. They're born sayin' "me first." They expect a woman to service 'em any old time he feels the goad, and if she can't, by God, he'll abuse her worse'n any animal in unnatural ways.

Animals are decent compared to a man.

That's about the only good thing you can say about Wayne, he's decent. But he ain't steady. If I could get him to walk the chalk, I'd swear he had *huevos de oro* like balls of gold, but he don't and he won't. Always off chasin' the rainbow, got to help an old partner get up on his feet again, got to do this, do that, but what about his wife?

Doesn't he know it's not proper to go rambling off on some mission of mercy and let the wife set at home waiting so it seems forever?

She found the ax, a chopping block, and a pile of mesquite limbs in the back and commenced chopping stove-length firewood.

"Hey, there!" An old woman in a shapeless dress over a shapeless body came tottering out. Her ankles were swollen to the size of her legs, and there was a yellowish gray tinge to her complexion that looked like death to Kate.

"Hey, there," the old lady repeated, "that ain't proper work for a lady."

"No, it ain't," Kate said, "it's proper work for a man."

"My man, he gets the rheumatiz if he works any. It's better to keep him off his feet so he don't complain so much." The old lady frowned at Kate, gathered up an armload of firewood, and trudged back into the torrid kitchen.

Massive Shig Radiguet and Bletcher stopped for a glass of beer in Gila Bend, having sweated out a gallon hard-riding their horses up the trail.

Shig asked the barman if he'd seen a man of

Wayne Carrol's description pass by, but the barman was no help.

"Never came in here. I never forget a face—"

"I heard you," Shig cut him off. "Likely he cut across."

"He'd be lucky to come out the other side. Damned few do," the barman said decisively. "They's skeletons out there never been found. Even Injuns. If the sidewinders don't get you, the scorpions will, and if they don't, then you just fry your brains out so you can't work again."

"That happen to you?" Shig laughed, and slapped Bletcher on the back.

The barman looked up into the bristled, greasy face of the big marshal, and over at the bullet-headed Bletcher, and then looked down at the bar. He didn't have enough nerve to go for the sawed-off two-bore right in front of him under the bar. He wished he did. He pictured himself raising the deadly shotgun, pulling the first trigger and blowing the marshal's head clean off his neck so there'd just be a stub gushing blood and crowin' like a short-chopped rooster, then swinging to the right and catching the paunchy Bletcher low, tearing his guts out and busting him in two.

But he didn't move except to swab the bar, and watch the greasy towel go around and around.

"Lost your voice?" Shig laughed.

"No, sir," the barman murmured, thinking, well, I sure told him.

"There's a skinny kid with this Wayne Carrol maybe," Shig said, "and a lying whore. You see 'em?"

"No, sir," the barman said, remembering the cocky kid and that good-looking piece with him. They'd come through yesterday.

"You sure?" Bletcher growled.

He wanted to come back at them, but thought better of it. Best just act simple, and let 'em ride on none the wiser.

"That Carrol broke jail. He's a bad one," Bletcher said.

"I heard of him," the barman said quietly, thinking that everything he'd heard about Wayne Carrol was good. He'd never bullied anyone down, and there were stories of widows getting mysterious donations, and bankers being instructed in human kindness.

Maybe he ran outside the law, but looking at the greasy badge on Radiguet's salt-crusted shirt, the barman thought, I wish he'd'a stopped by and asked for help.

"He'd cut your throat for a dollar," Bletcher said, "and what he does to womenfolk is as bad as a man can do."

"We're goin' to hang him this time," Shig Radiguet growled.

"Likely you'd have to go out in the *mala país* for him," the barman said carefully.

"He'll be comin' out the other side, if that's

where he went," Bletcher said. "We'll catch him before he ever gets to Tres Cruces."

"Tres Cruces."

"He left a big cache of army payroll money over there," Shig growled. "He can't forget it and he can't leave it."

"That's a long ways," the barman said neutrally. "Suppose he's going around by way of California and Oregon?"

"He ain't," Bletcher said.

"It's none of my business," the barman said, "but if it was me and I figured you were close on to me, I'd try runnin' a trick on you."

"You would because you're a jackass," Shig said meanly. "Nobody runs nothing on us."

"Yes, sir," the barman said tightly, smiling to himself. "How'd he break jail?"

"None of your goddamned business." Shig slammed his fist on the bar. "C'mon, Bletch."

The barman didn't protest that they hadn't paid for the beer. He was glad it was from the bottom of the barrel and he would have thrown it out if those two hadn't showed up.

At McDowell they stopped again. Their horses were lathered with sweat, but they found no beer.

"I sell whiskey by the bottle." A hunched-over gnome of a man peered up at them.

"Give us a bottle."

"Five dollars."

"You see this badge?" Shig Radiguet blustered.

"Was you meanin' to trade me that badge for a bottle of whiskey, I'd need four dollars and eighty-five cents to boot." The hunchback grinned.

"Where's the damned bottle?" Bletcher asked.

"I got to have the money first to find it." The little man grinned again. "I'm maybe just a nothin' of a man, but I go by the rules, same as you."

"I ought to beat your goddamned bald head with a gun barrel," Shig Radiguet growled.

"No, it won't do. If you ain't got the money, then I got to get over to the springhouse and set my brew."

The bowed-over little man crabbed toward the back door.

"Here's your goddamned five dollars." Radiguet threw the gold half eagle at the bartender's feet. "Now, bring us the goddamned bottle."

"Yes, sir." The bartender picked up the coin, looked at it doubtfully, but went on out the back door, returning presently with a bottle of yellow-stained white lightning, a film of fusel oil floating on top.

The hunchback put two glasses and the bottle on the plank bar and said, "Thanks, gents, for your custom."

"What is this stuff?" Shig Radiguet growled, pouring the clear liquid into his glass and passing the bottle on to Bletcher.

"Finest pure quill squaw whiskey west of the Big Muddy. It's so aged, I can't recall how long it's been." He cackled.

They drank, shuddered, glowered at the grinning little bald-headed man, and poured another.

"Looking for an escaped convict name of Wayne Carrol. Gray mustache, gaunted up some. Might be he's with a skinny kid and a whore with a good set of tits and a ass like a guitar."

"No. Never seen 'em. What's he done?"

"Strangled an old lady and violated her granddaughter," Bletcher laughed, unaware of the potency of the forty rod.

The little pink gnome of a man smiled broadly; his rubbery features seemed to be translucent, he was so pale.

"You an albino?" Shig Radiguet demanded.

"I'm about everything that God threw out the back door." The little man grinned. "Next time around, he promised me first lick of the ladle."

"You got any women around here?" Bletcher asked, the whiskey putting his mind on his manhood.

"You mean ho-gals? No, we ain't had a ho-gal since Big Nosed Lily and Dirty Lucy worked their way through. Goin' to California, they said, ridin' on their gold mines."

"They went through Fort Yuma about six months ago for the army payday, but they was like you, wouldn't give a sample without bein' payed in advance." Radiguet nodded, remembering.

From the front staging area came the sound of horses and wagons, and people gabbling.

"Wagon train from the East." The hunchback nodded. "They won't stay long. Likely they already watered their stock at the crossing."

Shig Radiguet strode to the open door and saw the Conestogas and spring wagons coming into the big empty area in front of the sutler's storehouse.

Climbing off one of the wagons was a man in a shiny black suit and a big woman with a lot of white bandages around her head.

They were arguing with the young couple who were coming down from the spring seat.

"It ain't our fault," the man in the shiny suit whined, "and we'll sure make it up to you soon as we reach California."

"I'm sorry . . ." the young man said, "maybe somebody else can carry you the rest of the way. . . ."

"You mean to set us afoot out here in the desert like we was lepers?" The woman stood tall, her bandaged head extended like an angry goose's.

"No, ma'am, it's just we only have so much, and it's all planned out day by day to last us through. If we carry you any longer, we won't make it past Fort Yuma," the young man tried to explain.

"God sent us to you, and God will reward you." The man smiled.

"I'm awfully sorry for your condition," the young man said, "but . . ."

"You eat twice as much as us," the young lady said straight out.

"Are you begrudging the unfortunate a crust of

bread?" the big woman asked sharply. "Is that what you're asaying?"

"We're just saying we hope you'll share your-selves out with the other folks," the young man stammered.

Shig Radiguet grinned as he saw the other folks purposely staying away, their backs turned, trying to look busy.

"We're on our honeymoon," the young lady said.

"The prophet of Nariz don't care about your slut-tish ways," the woman said, "if you reproduce. You mean to reproduce, don't you?"

"I can't see that concerns you. What concerns me is that somehow you ate up all the dried apples."

"Girl, I'm a missionary of the prophet Nariz," the woman said, "and I mean to see his word is honored."

"I guess we'll be going on," the young man said. "You'll be safe here."

"You can't abandon us in this wasteland!" the man moaned. "All we want is a ride. We'll beg off the others for food."

"My animals are already suffering some. We're carryin' too much weight. You can rest here until the stage comes by. It'll be easier and faster."

"There's no money," the woman growled. "If you could loan us twenty dollars, we'll send it right back to you soon as we reach the mission in Los Angeles."

"Don't do it," the young lady said, as the young

man seemed to wilt under the big woman's hot glare. "They can work."

"There is a place in hell reserved for those who serve mammon," the man in the shiny suit said.

"Wagons ho!" came the cry from on down the line.

"We're goin' with you." The woman set her foot on the hub of the wagon, meaning to heave herself up into the bed, when a sugar sack tied with twine fell from under her dress to the ground.

"There's our apples, Charles," the young bride said to her husband.

Charles picked up the bag of dried fruit and tossed it into the wagon.

"They ate most of 'em already," the young bride sniffed, and climbed up into the spring seat.

"Next time I play the good Samaritan," the young man said, "it'll be snowin' in Hades."

Mounting to the seat, he cracked his whip emphatically, and the team moved forward.

"Ingrates!" the man shouted. "You'll be punished!"

"I watched you!" the woman shouted. "I know what you're doin' and God knows too. He's watchin' you day and night out in the grass or under the covers!"

The wagons went by with their occupants studying another part of the landscape, and when the yard was empty, except for the outraged missionaries, Shig Radiguet stepped out into the heat.

"Looks like hard times." He nodded.

"The prophet Nariz is testing us," the man in the shiny suit said.

"Could you spare us a dollar for something to eat?" The big woman held out her hand.

"No, ma'am. I get twenty-four dollars a month for risking my life twenty-four hours a day; it don't go far enough for charity."

"Twenty-four dollars is just for the license to steal," she said firmly, her hand not moving back.

"Where you folks from?" Shig ignored the hand.

"Ohio," the man said. "Brother Jones saw the vision out there in his cornfield. Saw the prophet Nariz walking down the golden stairs with the tablets in his arms."

"That don't concern me none," Shig said, as the woman finally withdrew her hand, glaring at him hatefully. "What happened to your head?"

"A viper of a child tried to gun me down," she said, as if ready to weep.

"I'm sorry I asked," Shig said, starting to move back onto the bar. "Lucky he missed you."

"The little polecat, he took our horse and just left us to make our way out of Red Butte," the man said.

"What'd he look like?" Shig Radiguet turned back.

"A skinny kid about sixteen. Mean, sassy tongue. I'd like to jump down his throat and gallop his insides out."

"What about the man with the gray mustache?"

The two looked at each other with a mixture of fear and greed. How should they play the card, or should it just be denied? Never had it, never saw it, don't want it anyway.

"Last we seen him was out there in that desert full of burning red rocks."

"Alive?" Radiguet asked, trying to gauge how much they were lying.

"He was alive, but not by much. Why you askin'?" the man in the shiny suit asked, scratching at the stubble on his greasy jowls.

"He's an escaped killer."

"I knew it. I seen the evil in him," the woman said.

"Is there a reward? Some kind of bounty?" the man asked plain out.

"Not if he's dead," Shig said. "If I can take him alive, there's a hundred dollars for you."

"Would you mind giving us half in advance?" The man smiled.

"Yes. I'd mind," Shig growled. "Tell me the truth or you'll end up in Fort Yuma breakin' rocks."

"Not me," the woman said.

"You might like it." Shig leered. "Some of them cons is built like bulls, and they been starved from normal relations a long time."

Bletcher staggered to the doorway and looked from one to the other with muddy eyes.

"What's going on?"

"Filling up the penitentiary," Shig guffawed. "Woman here likes apples."

"God and the Prophet never forget and the mills of heaven grind the sinners into fine dust," the missionary declared. "The fact is, that man was dead when we found him out there. We made it back on his horse."

"Pretty good yarn, but I just think old Carrol is tougher'n any horse I ever saw." Shig laughed, the liquor lifting his spirits. "How about it, old girl, wanta make a dollar?"

"Satan, get thee hence!" the woman said, and dragged her husband away into the shade of the stage station.

"Was goin' to let her bite the apple off the tree," Shig laughed, "but she's already filled up."

"Damn, if she was just halfway good-lookin', I'd feed her a couple pounds of pork!" Bletcher hooted.

They had another drink and went through their limited imaginations as to how they would use the big woman if she didn't look like such an ox, and then Shig remembered Red Butte Station.

"He's over there right now," Shig muttered. "Maybe four hours."

"Let's go get him, then. . . ." Bletcher said, his eyes nearly closed.

"Better just follow him along till he digs up the cache. We take him tonight, all we got is a body."

"That's smart, old pardner." Bletcher belched,

coughed, then went out the back door and threw up.

Staggering back inside, he found a dark corner and lay down on the hard-packed dirt floor.

Shig Radiguet pondered the world by himself. The bartender had wisely departed. The bottle was still half-full. Eyes closed, Shig searched for it with his hand, finally found it, tilted it to his lips, and took a long swallow.

"Bring on the dancing girls!" He staggered about the empty, low-ceilinged room. "I'm ready to rip and howl!"

The long deep red flooded up from the great plain, submerging the butte which in that final light rose as a dark, lurid monument aglow as if a fire were burning inside.

The two riders came slowly across the flatland. Tyson tried to stay a little behind his father, because Wayne was slipping away, his face falling into the horse's mane, then grabbing ahold and jerking back as if nothing had happened.

Proud old devil, Tyson thought, won't admit he's beat down to doll rags.

Wasn't much you could do. Ride it out. At least he wasn't going to die of thirst or hunger. He might die of pride and muleheadedness, but Tyson could do nothing to change that.

What did he mean when he was rambling on about "the Cache"?

No doubt he was going for it wherever he'd cached it. Might be something he put away when he was rustling mavericks down in Texas twenty years ago, or maybe a sack of nuggets he'd took off a stage in Idaho last year. It was strange because he'd never known the old man to ever cache anything, always living day by day.

"Keeps you alive and in motion," he'd say when you'd mention there wasn't any money left in the sugar bowl.

So he'd never hidden out anything in his whole life. How come he's talking about the Cache now? Maybe he meant cash, but Tyson didn't think so. That would be too simple and easy for him.

No, it's something hid out and it's so strong in his mind, he lets it out when he's battered down.

Tyson couldn't think of anything that could be that strong in the old man's mind. It sure as hell wasn't money. He'd proved what he thought about money enough times.

But what else could it be?

Sometimes when he was feeling good and relaxed, he'd talk about the dream ranch he was looking for or sometimes he'd get dreamy about various extrafine horses he'd owned or stolen or tried to steal but failed, but they weren't any of them named Cache.

It didn't make much difference, Tyson decided; whatever it was, he'd give it away to some pilgrim with a sad story, forgetting he had a family at home

105

that wouldn't mind a few new blankets or some extra shakes on the roof, or a new-style mower to cut the hay instead of the man-killing cradle scythe.

Course, he could count on a meal almost anywhere he went because word had spread he was a giver instead of a taker; that is to say, he took from the bankers and the exploiters and the army, and anyone else stealing from the new country on an organized basis, but he'd never rob a prospector who'd brought a fortune in gold out of the mountains by his own pluck and sweat.

The people understood that kind of a man. They mostly all wanted to be the same way, but here's where they separated the sheep from the goats. Few of them would have guts enough to take a gun and use it in the first place. Second, if they happened to get away with some thousands of dollars, they'd put it in bonds or real estate or buy a new buggy to impress the neighbors.

Old Wayne, he never changed. Always wore clean blue jeans and chambray shirt. Never had a gold watch chain, nor even a tin watch. Had a pair of slick bull-hide chaps with a couple buckles broke, and a buffalo robe for winter made by an Indian woman for him. Had his name on it in little glass beads.

And then, he always rode the top horse in the country wherever he went, not just because it was a necessary tool in his trade, but because he had a true kinship with horses that went past buying and selling them. He liked them smart first, then he liked them strong, then he liked them fast. Give him the horse and an outfit and a new Remington .44 and he was in pig heaven.

How the hell he held up under the years was the miracle. He must be close to forty, but he never seemed to change much except for a few more gray hairs in his mustache.

Most men his age were settled down and going gray in the face, saying good-bye to life already, admitting it was all over, the roses gathered, the family started, what more did the world want from a man?

But old Wayne always acted like he hadn't yet found what he was looking for, but what he had found so far was something new and wonderful. Maybe it was a new horse, or a new territory to live in, or maybe a new woman; whatever, it was never the complete answer that he thought was due for him to discover if he kept at it long enough.

In that way, he could smile and dream and keep his shoulders back.

But what a rotten father he'd been. Most kids had a dad at home to make them study and learn from schoolbooks, but all Tyson knew was the ass end of a cow or a horse, and it took him three minutes to make his name on a piece of paper.

One of these days, he thought, I ain't waitin' no more for you to make up your mind, I'm going off and stick up my own bank and buy myself a schoolhouse.

He saw the figure in the dusk slump again over the horse's neck, and then he heard him say, "Cache. Cache, we comin' . . ."

Kneeing his mount close by, Tyson asked softly, "What's the Cache?"

The old man awakened and snapped to warily.

"What's that you say?"

"Cache what?"

"Soon as you're growed up enough to get along with folks, maybe I'll think up an answer to that," Wayne said, and smiled. "You're doin' better all the time."

"I don't give a damn about doin' better, and I don't need nothin' from you neither," Tyson said.

7

"WE'RE ALL TRAVELIN' TOGETHER FROM NOW on?" Kate's voice had a sharp edge on it and she wasn't exactly making it a question.

"Katie, if I go inside a bank with an empty bag, I don't figure to have you along," Wayne said.

He wasn't looking quite as old as he had a few hours before, Kate thought. The lump on the back of his head had gone down, and he'd found his smile again. A man with a smile always looks ten years younger than he is, and twenty years younger than a man with a bad mouth and hate in him.

"I can hold the horses."

"I reckon you could, but it ain't my custom." Wayne smiled.

"You can change," Kate said firmly.

"Up until you sent that fool telegram, I never saw the inside of a jail. That says something for my custom," Wayne said.

"If you'd paid attention to that telegram, you'd never been caught because you wouldn't'a done it."

"But dear little sweetheart," Wayne said patiently, "don't you see, they got the telegram and I didn't know anything about it."

"I don't see why," she said stubbornly. "The Western Union is supposed to deliver the telegram to those they're sent to."

"But you see, dear little trumpet vine flower, there's another big world out there you don't know nothing about."

"It's not my fault you didn't tell me you were famous."

"Ladybug, it ain't my job to tell my wife I'm famous. It's her job not to meddle in her husband's business which she don't know nothing about."

"I would if you'd tell me."

"If I told you, then you'd be as guilty as me in the eyes of the law, and I don't aim to have any wife of mine behind bars."

"It'd be better'n setting around a rented farm worrying as to whether you was dead or alive."

"Sweetie, little gingersnap, I have a plan. It's a good plan," he said slowly and carefully, "but if too many people hear about this plan, it won't ever happen."

"I don't ever talk. You know that."

"Ma'am, you send telegrams, you argue over pennies with the livery stable, you make yourself show up like Pikes Peak when we're supposed to be looking like little trees in a big woods. You just don't understand my business, and I don't see any reason you should."

"It ain't right you should be riding all over the western half of the United States while I'm to set on a rented hay farm in Kansas," she said determinedly.

"I can see that now." He nodded. "But you could have been doing your chores instead of bothering your head about me."

"I did all the chores in about half an hour."

"Next time, I'll leave you on a big spread with a stage stop and rooming house on it." He smiled.

"Won't be a next time. If there is, it'll surely be the last, I give you my word on that."

"Now, don't get yourself all fashed up into a lather that ain't needed," he replied quietly. "Best we all ride toward Tres Cruces pronto. We'll work it out from there."

"Why don't you tell me?"

" 'Cause I promised myself I wouldn't."

"Why'd you do that?"

"Because if it don't work, I don't want you disappointed. And I don't want the boy to think I failed him again."

They were lying in the darkness on a little rise about a hundred yards from Red Butte Station, a spot Wayne had picked after he'd had something to eat and a little rest. She'd argued it was safer sleeping on the floor of the main house, but he'd have none of it.

"We'll let the boy sleep in there and give us warning should that marshal come prowlin'," he'd insisted. "It don't do to sleep where anybody knows where you are."

"That's crazy," she'd argued.

"Lady mouse," he'd responded, "they's been more good bank robbers killed in their bedrooms than in banks."

He'd looped a hair rope around to discourage rattlesnakes, and then lay down on the blanket and looked up at the darkening sky.

"Sure good to be back with you," he'd said, and closed his eyes.

She lay with him, and cradled his head on her breast, and patted his shoulder to comfort him, but she couldn't keep quiet. She wanted to get it settled once and for all, and she couldn't wait till next week or even tomorrow.

All her pent-up feeling of abandonment and resentment rose up in her, and there was no way she could keep a lid on it. She was still snuggling up to him and patting his shoulder, but her body was tense and her mind unable to realize how terribly tired he felt.

Even as she was jabbering away at him, she heard him snore.

Darn it, she'd meant to set him straight, and then fool around some, and then make love, and then sleep.

Her first thought was to jab him in the ribs and wake him up so he'd promise not to roam anymore, but her good sense intercepted her impulse, and she smiled at herself in the darkness.

A good man is hard to find, she knew better'n most, and he was the best man she'd ever met except for his muleheaded independence.

Yet even that, most times she was proud of him for it, especially now that she knew he was famous, but heck, he ought to share himself a little extra because she needed a little extra to put the past behind and the future right up front.

He wouldn't even share the plan he had. She reckoned he'd rode alone so long, he couldn't do nothing else but hold his cards right on his vest and never let an eyelash flicker whether he was busted or had four aces.

Then he had his sidekicks off somewhere. They must have some way of passing messages, because he expected to meet them somewhere around Tres Cruces day after tomorrow.

Would they toll him away again? What kind of men were they? Who was the boss of the outfit?

For all she knew, Wayne was just a horse holder or lookout amongst some real bad men.

She kicked herself mentally for not knowing anything about the outlaw business except what she'd read in *Harper's Monthly.*

Up until she'd met Wayne, she'd thought outlaws were dirty, cruel, vicious men full of hate and the devil. Now she wasn't sure. Maybe Wayne was an exception to the rule, a freak outlaw who was good-hearted, and could make a joke every once in a while and worry about his family like he should.

Maybe Leonardo and Frank were bloodthirsty whoremasters.

The stars came out of the purple velvet sky as the pale yellow light in the west soaked into the shadow, and she patted his bony shoulder, thinking the first thing was to start feeding him up some.

Young Tyson hadn't spread his blanket on the floor like he was supposed to. Instead, as soon as they'd taken off to the rise, he took his blanket out to the bench in front of the mud and rock building and just sat down, taking in the coming of night, a magic time for almost anyone in the open country.

Here there wasn't a neighbor in twenty miles, so your eye couldn't be disturbed by somebody's coal oil lamp off somewhere. There wasn't anything except the heat rising back out of the earth and melting away into the cool night, then the first stars, then the moon that seemed as friendly as a grinning baldheaded Swede.

He was trying to find an answer to a problem he couldn't put into words. It was something to do with doin' right.

Somewhere along the line he'd been taught to do right. And that meant being respectful to your folks and keeping clean and doing your share of the work, and not eating any more than anybody else if there wasn't enough on the table.

He was thinking he'd been doing right as long as he could recall, but it didn't seem to get him anywhere. In fact, he seemed to be losin' ground.

It seemed like his dad was burned-out and goin' crazy, buttin' his head against a stone wall, and wouldn't trust him.

Got himself caught and sent to the pen, and then befriended those missionaries out there, and nearly got himself killed. For sure the old man was losing his grip and was headin' for a fall.

He was always trustin' people and being polite and then he'd get his tail caught in a crack, and his family had to make up for it.

And he wouldn't listen. Tried to tell him to quit bein' so danged nice and think about making a stake. Not for me but for his old age, which is on him right about now.

What's he goin' to do when he can't stand the long rides and privations after a bungled bank robbery, say? Well, you either die or set it out behind bars, which is about the same thing, only worse.

What was he trying to tell himself?

Maybe he should just ride off, so at least the old man couldn't use him for an excuse to go on robbin' banks and stages and payrolls.

Cut him right off at the pockets. Let him take care of Kate and settle down to a rockin' chair on the front porch somewhere.

None of it made sense. Everyone hated him, he thought, watching the stars, because he wouldn't back down from any of them or take any of their applesauce anymore. Well, let it be that way. He didn't need anybody. All he needed was his old six-gun and a good horse, and he'd show the old man somethin' about gatherin' in the money.

Took some skookum, though, to ride across that *mala país.* Or else that was just another part of his brain softenin'.

Walked the wrong way till past noon. That ought to show how he'd gone downhill. Man has to be *loco* to walk backwards.

One thing, no matter what anybody else thinks about me, any horse I can touch knows I'm his friend. There ain't a horse anywhere that don't know I'm doin' right, and that I know how he feels. Dad's a fair rider, but he'd never crawl under the belly of his horse, and I can do it crosswise and front to back, don't make any difference to me.

That horse ain't goin' to kick me because he knows I'm on his side.

He knows I ain't goin' to whip him, and I ain't goin' to spur him. I ain't goin' to hit him between the eyes with my fist or a club, and I ain't goin' to run him into the ground and shinbuck him, and I ain't goin' to notch his tailbone nor crop his ears. All I'm goin' to do to that horse is feed him the best grub I can find, and ride him so he feels smart, and rub him down so he feels proud to be my horse. Every horse I ever had would come when I whistled.

Not like the crazy people in the world, trying to ride the buck out of you before you can even get yourself set. They just want to cut and brand you, put you in a team, and send you out in harness haulin' freight for somebody else. Hell, I want to buck and run.

In this way, young Tyson tried to find himself in a time when he felt that he'd lost all guidance, that he'd been cast out, ready or not, and would have to make his own way because his stepmom wasn't really family and his dad wasn't smart enough to teach a settin' hen to cluck.

Not having friends his own age, he had no way of knowing that every sixteen-year-old boy in the country had similar thoughts of rebellion and despair, and disappointment that his father was hardly competent enough to put his pants on in the morning.

The difference between Tyson and the rest was that he was half horse, trail-wise, and carried a gun.

In the night, when infinity was traced out by the slow-wheeling stars and wise men and mathematicians tried to understand from opposite viewpoints just what it all signified, the land itself rested and opened a night world of ringtailed cats, kangaroo rats, and hungry owls calling for supper.

Oblivious to the stars or the rising moon, Shig Radiguet and Bletcher lay on cots in a small lean-to attached to the stage station and grumbled drunkenly.

"Goddamn it, I could peg a Siwash squaw tonight."

"I could peg a damn knothole," Bletcher responded, "but there ain't a goddamn nauch nowhere."

"That big missionary."

"I'd plug her up, but I have a feeling she ain't had a wash since the flood."

"Hold your nose."

"You're welcome. Tell me about it after you're done."

"I'd work her three ways," Shig said boozily.

"And likely she'd bite your pizzle off before you ever got to number two," Bletch giggled.

$$= 8 =$$

LEONARDO FAJARDO, LIKE ALL VAQUEROS, possessed a certain lassitude which could be called slackness or laziness, but in reality was an immense calmness which could not be changed except in a matter of life and death when a cowboy's skill could save a person's life. He could smile, he could frown, he could feel pain, but these were always on the surface. Behind those feelings, like a mountain behind the sculpture of a man's face, was this profound dimension that accepted weakness, strength, morality, and immorality, all as a piece of the same unwinding ribbon.

Most people never saw that dimension in the small, nondescript Mexican vaquero, a man wearing baggy pants under scarred chaps, a loose shirt, a greasy, scarred old hat, and star-heeled boots.

This plainness had its advantages. Leonardo Fajardo hardly looked like a man who held up stages, banks, and army payrolls.

He wore a worn Remington .44, but it fitted so well into his generally common attire, it was hardly noticeable.

The inscrutable calm inside the man was realized only by his closest friends and, of course, by all horses and most cattle.

Frank McCloud, Leonardo's sidekick, was solid

enough, but not in the same way as Leonardo. He was more like a hardwood stump rooted close to the ground and hard to knock over.

He wore a soft, flowing mustache, and above his broad, ruddy face his straight yellow hair was thinning out already so that his forehead seemed an extra size too big.

He was quick in his movements, but he lacked Leonardo's easy grace. Being so unalike, they were closer than brothers because their courage and loyalty had been tested many times since they'd first worked cattle at the Tejón Ranch in California's San Joaquin Valley years and years before.

The morning Frank got bucked off amongst some wild Sonoran steers had sealed their friendship. Both boys had been given green-broke horses because they were at the bottom of the ladder and it was thought that they should bear more troubles than the older vaqueros.

All except one of the long-legged, big-horned critters had veered away from the downed yellow-haired boy, but the one, a brindle devil, turned to hook Frank, who was still dazed from his fall.

Without hesitation, although he knew his colt was spooky and might buck, Leonardo drove him forward into the longhorn's shoulder, knocking him over.

The longhorn scrambled to its feet and made another pass at Frank, who was trying to capture his horse, and Leonardo gathered his colt once more and drove him against the big steer, knocking him down again.

That was enough for the steer, and in a minute the incident was just a little comical memory they could chuckle about, but Frank knew that the steer's needle-sharp horns had missed his belly by a whisker and had Leonardo hesitated, he would be buzzard bait.

When winter came on, they left the Tejón Ranch and drifted east along the border where it was warm, and the señoritas torrid.

All three had forgotten exactly how they came to meet in El Paso, where Wayne was watching his back and waiting for an idea. He'd meant to be whooping it up with a saddlebag full of gold pieces that he'd taken from the strongbox of a money-lender named George Veitengruber—done a good job of it too, nobody hurt and clear sailing ahead—when he found himself being fed sauerkraut and ponhaws, and talking to a German farmer about his crops.

The farmer had explained that Veitengruber had persuaded a bunch of them to come to south Texas to form a German colony of which he was the head. For the price of the third-class boat ride, they'd indentured themselves for five years to Veitengruber, and somehow they were getting deeper and deeper in debt to their master.

In short, Wayne Carrol had given the farmer the saddlebag and told him to buy everybody's freedom. He figured to come back in a month or so and pick up the money again, but for the moment he'd lie low in El Paso.

The three of them came back, all right, but George Veitengruber had put his money in the bank, and the bank was more like a fortress than a place of business so that they had to settle for the week's receipts and skedaddle out of Texas.

Of course, being young and full of pepper, they liked to gamble some and pursue the *chiquitas* to some extent, but none of the three could be called a low-down boozing, cheating womanizer. Neither were they ripstaving hellions, they were just three pretty much homeless cowboys on the drift.

Naturally Wayne, being a few years older, had a son back east somewhere, and he always sent a share of the plunder back to pay the boy's way.

It had been a pleasant, gentle time for them. Once in a while they'd ride with a herd or work on a ranch that was shorthanded because they'd all get sick of town food and gossip, late nights, and generally unhealthy atmosphere. It was as if they had to touch the ground every once in a while to remind themselves they were really just average to good human beings.

The one thing Wayne, Leonardo, and Frank feared most was that they'd get a reputation as man-killing gunfighters. They'd seen how a brand like that could ruin a man faster'n any vice so far invented.

They did everything but run to keep from gun-fighting, often going down El Paso's streets deliberately unarmed.

In time it was understood by the lowest of the outlaw elements in El Paso that these men were peacemakers more than bloodthirsty lunatics, and a kind of respect was granted them.

The bullies, even when drunk and on the prod, with a show of gallantry, hunted for easier game, and while the three gained a reputation for being outside the law, they were still honored for being generous and quiet-mouthed about it.

The Germans never forgot Wayne's contribution to their freedom, and there were other cases where honest, hardworking citizens were saved from an unholy corruption by the easygoing robbers.

In that way Wayne, and to a lesser extent Leonardo and Frank, became famous, but not for how many notches they'd carved, but rather for their honest workmanship and general clearheadedness.

Usually Wayne drifted off somewhere alone after a successful holdup, but they'd arrange a future meeting place before he left, and when he came back, they'd go looking to make some money.

So it had been set up that they would meet not in Tres Cruces as Shig Radiguet had been led to believe, but in Agua Prieta, a friendly Mexican border town farther south.

The slim vaquero Leonardo and the fair-haired chopping block Frank rode down Agua Prieta's unmemorable one-block main street at a walk. The mud buildings were ugly, dusty, populated by families of several generations as well as their chickens, goats, and pigs. There was a cantina with a rooming house next to it. On down the street was a *tienda* that sold general merchandise in very small quantities. If you wanted a piece of paper, the old lady would tear it off a tablet and ask a penny for it.

If you wanted one .45-caliber cartridge, she would take one out of the box and sell it to you for double its worth.

They stopped in front of the rooming house and arranged for two cots and care for their horses, and with the sun beating down on the dusty, nearly empty street, they strayed off into the cantina, which consisted of a plank bar, no stools or spittoons, but three or four tables with chairs made of *palo duro* and laced with rawhide. A boy, on seeing them, hurried out into the backyard where his mother was washing clothes in a boiler next to a corncrib. She in turn sent the boy on to another mud shack, where he informed his father that there were two clients waiting.

A small, roly-poly man emerged wearing only a thin pair of pants and sandals. His hair was rumpled and his eyes still half-asleep.

Waddling in the back door, it took his eyes a few seconds to adjust to the darkness, but when he recognized the two men, he cried out, *"Amigos!"* and rushed around the bar, shaking hands, embracing Frank, clapping his shoulder three times, then stepping back to shake his hand again in the classic *abrazo*.

"*Qué tal? Como to va? Qué pasa?*"

Then he went through the same enthusiastic ritual with Leonardo.

Chattering greetings and asking questions about how was the trip and when did you get in, and such small things to make them welcome, the proprietor, whose name was Salomé, but who was called Chapo because he was short, made the pair wonder why they had ever left Mexico.

Remembering the surly gringo bar-dogs in Houston lording it over mahogany bars with mirrors and high-priced brandies, they realized that a little bit of human kindness went a long way.

"What can I get you? I have some beer in the well!" Chapo grinned. "I must have known you were coming. Pepe," he called to the boy, "bring up the beer from the well, three bottles."

"Yes, Papa." The boy scampered out the back door, and cranked up the windlass that held a tub of ceramic bottles with patented lock-down caps.

Fetching out three wet bottles, he let the windlass crank down again, and then brought the three bottles in to his father.

Unbuckling the rubber-washered caps, Chapo set a bottle in front of each man, then lifted his own. "*Salud.*"

The beer was not exactly cold, but Leonardo was pleased to be in a cool, dark place with good friends, the bubbling good humor of Chapo, as well as the visibly relaxing posture of his *compañero* Frank.

Frank had a tendency to get nervous during a long ride, as if the tiredness was telling him to watch more closely every little squirrel hole, or cholla cactus. Now he was grinning, his eyes alight with fun.

They finished the beer, and Chapo cried out, "Another!" The boy ran to the well, as Chapo repeated the old saying to Frank: *Una es ninguna, dos es una mitad, tres es una, y como una es ninguna, pues, una mas!* which Leonardo translated, One beer is nothing, so two are a half, and three is only one, and as one beer is nothing, let's have another!

But the beer was strong, and no one wanted to drink more than two in an afternoon, because after all, there could be no fiesta until Don Wayne arrived.

They explained to Chapo that Wayne had been imprisoned for the past eight months, and they only hoped he still retained his health.

"But how did it happen?" Chapo exclaimed. "You left here on good grain-fed horses, and with confidence."

"We don't know exactly," Frank replied. "The marshal had advance word we were coming."

"We'd just got the payroll out of the wagon, when here he comes with a bunch of others. They didn't mean to take any prisoners."

"*Claro!*" Chapo said to continue the story.

"We ran north into the mountains, but they were too close on us and Wayne's horse was hit."

"He insisted we run on, and lie low in Houston until we heard from him."

"He kept the posse pinned down from behind his dead horse," Leonardo said, "so we could get loose."

"But how long did this take?" Chapo asked, his eyes wide with wonder.

"They were after us for two days. Wayne scouted ahead of us, but there was no way out except by the pass coming out toward Morenci, then they shot Wayne's horse. That's all we know."

"The payroll, may I ask?" Chapo asked timidly.

"It is safe where it is," Leonardo said quietly but firmly, closing the subject.

"He held them off for you. That is his way," Chapo said, and lifted his brown mug. "*Salud a Don Wayne,*" he intoned solemnly. "May he arrive safely."

In that way they sipped a little beer during the day, had a plate of pork stew and corn tortillas, napped afterwards, and were not surprised as the shadows lengthened to see Wayne riding a leggy chestnut down the street. The surprise was that he had two companions, his young wife and his son, riding along with him.

"What does it mean?" Frank worried.

"It means," Leonardo said, "that always with Wayne, nothing's ever as before."

"He looks like he's been beat to a dime's worth of dog meat. Lord, he's thin," Frank whispered.

"Yuma is famous for changing a man's appearance."

When the three riders came abreast of the cantina, most of the town had recognized Wayne and hurried out into the street to greet him. Frank, Leonardo, and Chapo followed along, smiling, feeling good that they were back together again. The crowd surrounded Wayne and left Kate and Tyson outside the circle.

"Buenos Días! Bienvenidas, Don Wayne. Con mucho gusto!"

After the *abrazos* and the greetings of welcome, it was "How is your family?" and Wayne presented Kate and Tyson, then asked Chapo in return, "How is your brother Enrique in Tres Cruces?"

"Bien, bien!" Chapo smiled.

Kate stared in wonder that her husband could have such an enthusiastic group of friends, and Tyson thought the old man had paid them all off, bought their friendship with stolen money, and he could have just as many friends whenever he cut loose on his own.

More cots were arranged under the brush arbor in the courtyard of the rooming house, and Chapo's wife insisted on fixing them a full-scale stewed chicken dinner even though it was very late.

After seeing to the horses, they washed up and sat down to supper.

"We've been out of touch," Frank said to Wayne.

"Problem is that marshal from Yuma," Wayne said, filling his bowl with the rich chocolate-flavored mole sauce and a chicken breast. Using a corn tortilla as a spoon, he ate ravenously.

"Got to fill up a big canyon in my middle." He smiled, and seeing Tyson staring curiously about, said happily, "By golly, it's good to be here! What do you think, Ty?"

"How much did it cost you?" Tyson asked.

Wayne hid his feelings and pretended to take a moment to think. "I don't recollect anybody in this town ever asking me for anything. Course, the women always want flower and vegetable seeds, and I've brought what I could."

"You think they just like you?" Tyson asked cynically.

"Tyson," Kate put in, warning.

"It's all right, Kate. He don't know it, but he's learning, and he needs to see some truth. Point is, son, you're eating a mighty fine dinner, and if you want to really insult a man, ask Chapo how much it costs."

"But he's paid in some other way."

"I look at it different. There's things they can't buy here. If I bring Mama some zinnia seeds, she's happy and I'm happy. If I can bring Chapo some beer bottles with patented tops, we're all happy. Now, lesson number one is that there ain't nothing wrong in being happy no matter how many holy men tell you otherwise."

"But these are your friends, not mine," Tyson said.

"No, they're yours too if you earn their friendship, but I can understand you want to make your own friends. I'm just tryin' to show you a way."

"I don't see it," Tyson said stubbornly.

"No hurry, son." Wayne smiled. "Once you get the hang of caring for other folks, it'll come easy."

"How long will we be here?" Kate asked.

"Tell the truth, Kate, I'm not quite up to my usual ring-tailed rooster condition yet, but another day of good chuck like this, and I think I can ride a ways."

"That's just what I want," she said. "You rest. Put some tallow on your bones. I'm worried sick about you looking like a critter that's starved to death."

"I don't feel the worse for the trip, now that I got my head back to normal," Wayne said. "Point is, we're just not in any hurry to do anything."

"Did you ever find out how they knew we were going to do business in Tres Cruces?" Frank asked. "I'd like to sweat somebody for that."

"Yes, well, I guess it was just somebody over-anxious to do me a favor," Wayne said carefully. "It's past history now."

Leonardo passively flicked his eyes about so quickly, everyone thought he was still half-asleep, but he'd seen the red rise in Kate's cheeks, and her lips tighten.

"Then we'll let it be," he said quietly. "Anybody followin' you?"

"Not directly on our tail," Wayne said thoughtfully, "but they're coming."

"They won't come across the border," Frank said.

"I don't know for sure about that big bastard, Radiguet. He's crazy enough to do anything. I hate to think of what he'd do if he ever went loco in this town."

"Best kill him," Frank said.

"Then what? There'd be ten more just like him."

"Let's go back to California. Maybe Tejón Ranch needs some punchers," Leonardo said. "I can train every *potro* on their range and have some fun doin' it."

"I've got somethin else on my mind, once we settle the back trail," Wayne said.

Kate watched his lean face anxiously, but she said nothing, because no matter what she said, he was going to do it his way.

Shig Radiguet with his sore-butted deputy arrived in Tres Cruces an hour after sunset.

Except for a few cattle ranches owned mostly by Mexicans, there was little of importance to Tres

Cruces except for its separate stage stop, which fed passengers going north and south as well as east and west.

An old town, it had grown on itself. The more people who stopped there and bought something, the more people could live there and sell their services. In that way, it had a mercantile, a hotel, a saloon, a barbershop, and a sometime doctor when he was sober. A mile down the trail with its own well was the gringo stage stop and telegraph office.

The people of Tres Cruces left the stage depot alone, and the stage people were hardly aware that there was a Mexican village nearby with its own simple government, including a sheriff. The people of Tres Cruces had been so humiliated at being considered less than human by the traveling gringos, they no longer offered a smile or their usual hospitality.

Radiguet and Bletcher, smelling of beer, sweat, vomit, piss pants, and foot thrush, were not welcomed when they strode heavily into the primitive restaurant.

The pair had stopped at the stage stop and downed half a bottle of forty rod on empty stomachs before continuing on.

It pleased Radiguet to show how filthy he could be. It showed he'd been on the trail a long time, and he was mean as a bagful of bobcats. It pleased him that a man was saying to his wife, "Look at the big dirty marshal."

Deliberately he brushed chairs aside as he swaggered to a table in the back as if they hadn't made the place big enough for a man of such bulk.

"Steak and onions and potatoes and gravy," he ordered from a shy Mexican girl named Maria.

Obviously she spoke little English and she stammered, *"Mandé?"*

As there were no other customers in the place so late in the day, there was no one to help her translate, and Radiguet felt mean enough to handle it his way.

"Steak and potatoes, stupid," he said, "and all the trimmings."

"Tell her, Shig!" Bletcher laughed. "Tell her I want her to smoke my cigar after supper."

"Not this little chili pepper," Radiguet said. "You go find your own, this one is mine."

"Mandá?" She trembled. She was near her sixteenth birthday. Her young breasts were high and firm, and her waist was slimmer than her hips, which stretched the faded skirt.

"Meat!" roared Shig Radiguet, his broken yellow tooth showing against the grainy stubble on his blocky face.

"Sí, señor," she said, comprehending only that she'd best go find her mother in the kitchen or her father asleep on the roof.

Backing away as Radiguet rose and advanced upon her, she shrieked like a mouse hypnotized by a snake, *"Mamá!"*

"Come here, you little bitch!" Radiguet grabbed at her and managed to catch a part of her flimsy dress, which tore as she backed off, revealing her nudity.

The rag of a dress still in his hand, Radiguet advanced on her as she backed into a corner.

Maria was trying to cover the glossy pubic hair that curled away from her firm rising mons, and at the same time cover her tiny nippled breasts with her arms.

"Go get her, man! Cut your wolf loose, Shig!" Bletcher hooted in a strange state of excitement, as Radiguet caught the girl around her slim waist and brought her to him, his left hand slipping down over her pert little bottom.

"Mamá!" Maria squeaked for the last time, as Radiguet bent down and planted his hirsute mouth on hers.

Mama emerged from the kitchen as Radiguet hoisted the paralyzed girl onto a table and was fumbling anxiously at the buttons of his fly.

Mama took one look and screamed loud and clear. "Enrique! *Socorro!*"

Goddamn it, I almost had her, Radiguet thought angrily, and then thought the hell with it, he'd still have her if it was the last thing he ever did.

Maria, given the moment to realize what was happening, tried to twist away from the big man, but he had her locked to him with his powerful left hand.

With a crazy laugh, Bletcher barred the way of Mama, a short woman with big breasts, a big butt, and a thick waist.

"This one's mine," Bletcher yelled, determined to hold up his end of the affair.

At this moment Enrique dropped down from the roof with an ancient fowling piece in one hand.

Rushing in from the front door, he saw the struggle of his women in the lamplight, and raised the long barrel to aim at Shig Radiguet, but he couldn't fire because his daughter was in the way. Shig quickly dropped his right hand to the butt of his Colt, drew and fired, his bullet taking the older Mexican in the chest, sending him staggering back into the night.

"Socorro!" the mama screamed, and rammed her knee into Bletcher's crotch, sending him slumping to one knee, his face pale gray, his cry a stifled moan.

"Socorro!" she screamed again, and Radiguet suddenly awakened to the fact that he had just shot a Mexican in a town where he had no friends.

Releasing the girl, he turned the gun on Mama and yelled, "Shut up!"

"Socorro!" she howled, uncaring, and ran to her fallen husband, while the girl darted into the kitchen and out the back door.

Mama's scream of sorrow and rage was even louder than her cries for help, and people began arriving on the run.

"Better get the hell outa here," Bletcher said huskily.

Still holding the six-gun, Radiguet said, "Yeah, c'mon," and marched out the front door where a small crowd of people were gathered about Enrique's body, all jabbering away in Spanish incomprehensible to his ears.

"It was self-defense! See the goddamned shotgun? He had no right!" he yelled loudly, and pointed at his badge. "I am the law. Understand? You can't shoot an officer of the law!"

"Why not?" someone asked quietly from the crowd, and Radiguet swung the Colt around, but he couldn't make out the speaker in the darkness.

"Como no?" came another voice behind him, and he felt a flicker of fear run up his spine into his back hair, and said, "Bastards! Let's go."

"If you got any complaint, you just tell it to your sheriff," Bletcher yelled at the crowd as he mounted up.

"No! We're going to tell Don Wayne Carrol," a voice called clearly from the darkness.

"Fine! Yeah! Do it! Tell Carrol I killed this old bastard and I'm goin' to kill him the same way. Tell him I'm waiting!" Radiguet roared, and jammed his spurs in his horse's flanks.

NEXT MORNING, KNOWING NOTHING OF THE tragic death of Enrique in Tres Cruces, Wayne suggested they pack up a couple burros for a round-abouty trip north.

"We can't show our faces around Tres Cruces just yet," Wayne counseled Frank and Leonardo.

"But where do we go?" Leonardo asked.

"It's just north and west of where they shot down my good horse." Wayne drew a map in the soft dirt with his finger. "The payroll's cached there out of the weather, but that ain't exactly what I'm after."

"You been there before?" Frank asked.

"Yes, two years ago I had a quick look-see. Like I told you when we was on the scat, there's only one way in or out. I went in, cached the money box, and came back out fast so's they'd not find it."

"What's so special about the place?" Tyson asked.

"I don't rightly know. I only seen a piece of it, and both times I was goin' at a gallop."

"That's all dry country up that way."

"Likely you're right. Maybe I was just ramblin' so fast, it looked green to me."

"It won't hurt to look," Frank said.

"When you do a bank job," Tyson asked, his thoughts elsewhere, "do you stick up the teller, or do you go get the president out of his office first?"

"Depends," Wayne said, cocking his head curiously. "Why?"

"I'm trying to learn the game." Tyson turned to face a pepper tree, then flashed his right hand down to the mended butt of his .45, drew swiftly, cocking the old piece as he brought it up.

"Son, you make me nervous playing with that old brute. Likely it'd blow out into your face iffen you popped a cap."

"Got to start somewhere," Tyson said.

"Don't start with that scrap iron. When I think you're growed-up and ready, I'll give you mine."

"You're always sayin' I'm too young!" Tyson protested, his eyes hot. "How can I grow up if I don't do something?"

"You're already way ahead of any kid your age," Frank said.

"Tyson, try to remember that your father is like one in a million. You can't just jump into his boots in the way other young men can jump into their fathers' boots. He is something special," Leonardo said.

"I'm tired of being treated like a weanling. Just because I ain't killed anybody yet don't mean I couldn't."

"It ain't killin' that makes a man better, it's savin' lives, savin' opportunities, givin' people a chance to make something of themselves," Wayne said, awkwardly searching for the right words, and feeling sweat break out on his forehead.

137

He'd known the boy was spooked some, but he hadn't known how far his imagination had carried him without the benefit of experience.

"You learned! Nobody got in your way and tried to hold you down!" Tyson shot back hotly.

"Tyson, listen to me a minute. There was the Civil War when I was your age. My folks had a farm in Pennsylvania and when the rebs come at us, I didn't have much choice but to grab a musket and start fightin'. When the battle of Gettysburg was over, there was fifty thousand dead boys layin' about. That's a bunch."

"So what are you sayin'?"

"Live a little before you have to grab a gun the way I did."

"I was some younger, son," Frank said, "but I had a brother same age as your dad. When Lee said charge up that hill, he charged, and he never came back."

"It is strange to say that the American George Walker attempted to take Baja California by capturing the capital city of La Paz. An old general named Altamirano, retired to his ranch at Todos Santos, gathered up his vaqueros, rode across the desert, and kicked the gringo out." Leonardo smiled. "I rode a burro after my father, carrying a machete almost bigger than me."

"So in a way, we all fought against each other before we even knew what the fightin' was about," Frank said.

"It ain't something you got to hunt down," Wayne said softly. "It'll come at you soon enough."

"And don't forget," Frank added, "it isn't always the best man, or the fastest draw, or the deadliest shot that wins. When folks start shootin' at each other, it gets to be a question of luck."

"Some have it, some don't, Tyson," Leonardo said.

"Well, dang it, how do I find out what I'm made of?"

"Have a little patience." Wayne put his hand on Tyson's thin shoulder. "Likely this cache valley I caught a fast glimpse of ain't worth peein' on, and we'll ride on south."

"Can we get a move on?" Frank said impatiently. "It ain't goin' to get any cooler off yonder."

The burros were loaded with supplies and bedrolls, and they were just finishing their coffee in the ramada with Chapo, saying their good-byes, when a young man in white trousers and tunic, riding a Spanish mule, galloped in from the north.

He was a cousin of Chapo and had ridden south to tell Chapo the bad news about his brother Enrique.

At first they spoke alone, out in the street, but soon the emotions were riding high, and Chapo came into the ramada, his back straight, his eyes afire.

"Qué pasa, hermano?" Wayne asked quickly.

"That man, that lawman, the big man who took you to Fort Yuma. He came to Tres Cruces last night with another man. Big too, but fat and oily."

"Bletcher," Wayne said softly, waiting.

"They tried to rape Enrique's daughter, and when he came to protect her, the marshal shot him dead," Chapo said, tears coming into his eyes.

"I'm so sorry," Wayne said.

"We'll take care of it," Frank said.

"No, he was my brother, and I will take care of it."

"You wouldn't have a chance against Shig Radiguet," Wayne said.

"The people told him you were coming," Chapo said.

Wayne considered the two things he had to do. One could be a positive step forward, the other was just more killing that would never end.

"I'm not going to Tres Cruces," Wayne murmured. "That marshal can wait."

Chapo looked at the weathered, gray-mustached man in surprise, then closed all expression from his face. "I will take care of it."

"No, I don't want you to. Keep them there in Tres Cruces," Wayne gritted. "It's just I got something else to do first."

"Dad—" Tyson said accusingly.

"C'mon, we're riding," Wayne said, knowing they all thought he was backing down, afraid of the big marshal, gotten old and lost his nerve.

It was in their eyes, and he didn't blame them. If he was in their boots, he'd think the same thing, but they didn't know what he knew, and once in his life he meant to do the right thing before it was too late.

Maybe it was already too late.

"I'll ride with you," Tyson said to Chapo, making it plain what he felt about his father.

"No, no, it will be taken care of by my own people," Chapo said. "You must obey your father."

"I said I'd handle it later," Wayne said, an edge to his voice, "and then I said, 'let's ride.'"

There were no farewell *abrazos*, no saying when you return, my house is your house. No, the little mud village seemed to close in upon itself as the five riders departed, leading the two heavily packed burros.

Wayne took the lead with Kate at his side.

"What's bothering you?" she asked after several miles of silent riding across the spiny desert.

"I can't explain it because I don't know what's ahead. I don't even want to know."

"You're going backwards today for sure."

"I want somebody to tell me after we get there," he said shortly. "If it don't happen, it don't. Then we'll go look for another bridge to cross."

"Or another windmill to charge against." She grinned. "You're not fooling me any, husband."

"I'm glad you have more confidence than me," he said.

"You don't have to prove yourself against Shig Radiguet."

"I never ever went against a man because I felt

short of skookum, but it seems like they're catchin' up with me."

"Who?"

"Them folks I hold dear who used to put their trust in me."

"Don't make up something that isn't there," she said.

"Oh, it's there. I ain't exactly blind yet, but I got other things on my mind."

"When are we going to settle down and laugh a little?" she asked lightly.

"Sweetie bun, you're just as pretty as a spotted pig in a flower patch, but I'm thinking we better be thinkin' about Tyson. He's slippin' off a cliff and don't even know it."

"He's just crowin' like a banty rooster," she said. "It's only a stage he's in. He'll grow out of it."

"Out here folks don't get too many chances to make serious mistakes," Wayne worried.

"You ever figure that Shig won't be settin' around town waiting for you?"

"Course. He wants the cache. We'll be plumb lucky if he ain't up there waitin' in the pass with about twenty hungry sharpshooters."

"That would solve all your problems. You could take down Radiguet and Bletcher, and the boy could smell some gunsmoke, and then we'd end up with the cache."

"Nothing like a fool girl to think up a fairy story." Wayne smiled thinly. "Most of these kind of affairs I've attended end up with the outlaws all dead and a couple marshals proppin' em up for their pictures. It's an ugly business that they don't tell you in the *Harper's Monthly*."

They stopped at noon under the shade of an old mesquite for dinner.

"Where you reckon we are?" Frank asked.

"About ten miles west of Tres Cruces. We'll cut the trail pretty soon," Wayne said. "I'd like for nobody to see us goin' by."

Tyson glanced at Wayne and wondered what he was so afraid of. Sure was something had cut him down to size. Ducking a challenge, refusing to avenge Chapo's brother, skulking along off the trails like he smelt worse'n a squaw on a gut wagon. Maybe that's what happened when you got old. You just lost your speed, forgot things, made mistakes, so you became afraid of any little mouse noise.

Tyson made up his mind that he never wanted to end up that way. Likely he'd be dead before he was thirty, but he'd have lived as hard as he could and he'd never suffer the shame of growing old.

If he had his way, he wouldn't be hiding out on a back trail. He wouldn't be looking for a hide-out canyon where there wasn't nothing but rattlesnakes and scorpions, he wouldn't even thinking about lying low when there was a man just ten miles off who ought to be faced and killed.

But instead of going into Tres Cruces and bein' a

man, they were worming their gutless way up into the hot, dry badlands where the mountains petered out.

Kate dropped back and rode alongside Tyson as if she wanted a change of company.

"You look lower'n a bull snake's belt buckle." She grinned. "What's on your mind?"

"Nothin' much," he muttered. "I'm bein' patient like everybody tells me. I been patient long as I can remember. Old folks always sayin', 'be patient, be patient.' Sure, I been patient, and the next thing you know, I'll be old and burned-out, saying be patient to some kid that has better things to do if he'd just get his guts up and do 'em."

"There's something goin' on that neither one of us knows about," Kate said in a low voice. "Your dad is a hard man to read."

"Maybe he's about as hard to read as an old work bull that never had nothin' to read in the first place."

"Give him a couple more days before you make up your mind," she suggested.

"You care a lot about him?" Tyson asked carefully.

"I married him and I'm damned glad," she replied.

"He must've been one of the big bears," Tyson said doubtfully, "but no more."

"You're thinking wrong," she murmured.

"He killed his first man in the war when he was sixteen. He said so. Now everybody tells me to be patient when there's a snake of a U.S. Marshal just an hour over that way I ought to be puttin' down."

"Wars are different. It isn't one on one. You don't know nothin' about the man you're killing. Could be your brother, you don't know. Why you so damned eager to shoot somebody?"

" 'Cause that's what I'm goin' to do, and I'd as liefer get started on it soon as I can, 'cause I won't be around past thirty if I'm lucky enough to make it that far."

"Oh, Tyson," she chuckled, "likely you'll be setting in a soft chair with a beard down to your knees tellin' tales to your grandchildren."

"Nobody, goddamn, takes me serious!" He set his jaw tight and tried to look like a killer.

"You'll grow out of it." She smiled and rode on back up to Wayne.

In a moment, Leonardo changed position, leaving Frank to bring the burros.

"Your dad teach you to ride?" Leonardo asked Tyson, making conversation.

"I guess he started me out," Tyson said.

"You got a good set." Leonardo nodded. "It comes natural. Some have it, some don't."

"How can you tell?" Tyson asked curiously.

"You see the rider first, of course. But then you look at the horse and not the rider. The horse has his head up, his eyes are looking around, he's having a good time. He's not being punched down by a lazy man, he's bein' lifted up by somebody that likes a horse better than anything. He's smiling, that's how."

"You trying to sell me something?" Tyson asked, wondering all of a sudden why everybody was being so damn nice to him.

Leonardo threw back his head and laughed. "No, *muchacho*, I'm passing the time of day, nothing else. Someday, though, if you like, I can show you some things about horses you may not know."

"Like what?" Tyson asked bluntly.

"Like patience is the greatest virtue in training a wild colt. It's not how much muscle you have, it's how well you can put up with his foolishness."

"I wanted to train a colt once, but Dad said we had to move in a hurry, and I had to leave him behind," Tyson said, setting his jaw again.

"There are others waiting for your touch." Leonardo smiled.

An hour before sunset, they had climbed into the mountains, following Wayne's lead as he picked out old Indian trails and game paths that led off into the formidable bare red crags, the same as the *mala país* except the rocks were big as mountains, and the gulches canyons.

There can't be any water out here, Tyson thought to himself. I just want to see the look on his face when he finally has to admit it.

They passed the bones of a horse lying on a wide bench where an obvious trail turned left.

Wayne called out, "We're not far."

"The big strawberry," Leonardo remarked to Frank as they rode by the bones. "Much horse."

"I can't figure why he's so set on coming all this way with everybody and pack burros besides," Frank said. "Hell, we could have rode up here from Agua Prieta, picked up the payroll, and been back by now."

"I know what you mean," Leonardo said, "but do you not see that he is carrying a mountain on his shoulders which he is trying to hide?"

"It ain't like him." Frank shook his head, disapproving.

The rock strata changed from red sandstone to a gray granite sometimes splashed with bright white quartz, and piñons perfumed the air. The cliffside trail narrowed, and a short distance ahead, it disappeared.

"It'll be hell turning those burros around," Frank muttered.

"He knows where he's going," Leonardo said hopefully, thinking that all they needed was for a horse to spook and they'd all be tumbling down the mountainside.

Suddenly Wayne disappeared.

"Holy Jesus!" Leonardo stared. Then Kate was gone, and as the boy followed in file, he too vanished.

In another step Leonardo saw the jagged fissure in the granite, concealed by a piñon that seemed to guard the diagonal cut.

"How the devil did he ever find it?" Frank exclaimed.

"Yes, ask the devil." Leonardo chuckled and turned his horse in to the portal, Frank following right behind him with the burros.

It was an unbelievable change. In a few feet they grouped together on a granite bench and looked down upon a green valley surrounded by high mountains.

"This is the only way in," Wayne said. "I passed by here, saw what you see, and decided to scoot back out again."

"Looks like a helluva place to hide out in," Tyson said, studying the long valley below. "Why'd you leave it?"

"I wanted to keep it hidden, and those lawmen were too close," Wayne said. "So I beat it back to the fork where Frank and Leonardo were waiting."

"You mean you took a chance on Fort Yuma or worse just to hide this valley?" Kate looked at Wayne in awe.

"Likely it wasn't worth it," he said humbly. "But a man looks for a place and maybe he finds it, maybe he doesn't. Still it's got to have its chance."

"Certainly if anyone in that posse saw this valley, there would be prospectors and horse hunters and grangers all over it now," Leonardo said.

"I just don't know," Wayne said heavily, and dismounting, walked off to a great monolith of granite, entered an eroded cave on the back side of it, and fetched out a leather box with brass trimmings.

"There she is, boys. We can split it and ride to Mexico, or put it back for safekeepin', whatever's your pleasure."

"I thought we were supposed to camp in your valley," Tyson said grumpily.

"Ain't mine," Wayne said. "I named it Cache Valley, because that's what it is, plain hid out, but it don't mean nothing to an old rambler like me. You folks just make up your minds and we'll head off for Hermosillo or California, whatever you say."

"My, you are talky all of a sudden," Kate said, staring at Wayne, trying to fathom why he was talking like a querulous old man now.

Plumb lost his mind, Tyson thought.

"Let's have a look, so long as we come all this way," Kate said decisively.

"I'm agreeable," Frank said.

"Of course," Leonardo said, standing in his stirrups and looking into the distant verdancy.

"What do you say, son?" Wayne asked wearily.

"I think we ought to ride to Tres Cruces and kill that marshal," Tyson said, quick-drawing his .45 and aiming at the money box. "After then, we can poke around all we want."

"You're outvoted," Kate said before an argument could start. "Maybe tomorrow we'll think on it some more."

"I'm sorry, son," Wayne said, putting the money box back in the cave.

"We have an hour to get into the bottom and set

149

up camp," Kate said. "You can make all the chin music you want then."

With Kate crowding behind him, Wayne led them on down a dog-legged trail that would have held back most horses, and crossed solid rock benches that stepped on down to the bottom of the valley itself.

Big ponderosa pines and oaks thrived, and a splashing stream rolled merrily through a meadow, belly-deep in grass.

"No Injuns," Frank said. "Ain't a smell of smoke or nothin'."

"I think they was here once, but something killed 'em. Maybe a Spaniard with the smallpox got in amongst 'em," Wayne murmured.

"It could happen," Leonardo said. "Every Indian on the Baja peninsula died when the Spanish arrived with their plague."

The men gathered wood for a fire, unpacked the burros, and hobbled them. Before sunset the camp was made and a cheery little cook fire was going.

Suddenly there was a rattle of loose rock from the other side of the valley that echoed back and forth.

"Something lives here," Kate said.

"Maybe bears," Wayne said. "If you don't mind, I'm goin' to take a little snooze."

Tottering off into the shadows, he found his bedroll, shucked his boots and hat, loosened his belt, and lay down.

The others looked at each other nervously over the fire.

"Ain't like him to quit early."

"Tired."

"I'm not feeling all that worn down."

"He's old," Tyson murmured. "Lost his grip."

"Might be."

"Don't forget he just got out of Fort Yuma," Kate protested in a whisper.

"Sure, that'd take a lot out of a man," Frank nodded.

"With age comes experience," Leonardo said.

"I reckon they don't have no homes for old owl-hooters like they do sailing men," Tyson said.

"Owl-hooters wouldn't go to no home," Frank growled. "When I get old, I want my bones to be picked by the coyotes like old Strawberry's up yonder."

"Not me," Leonardo grinned. "I want to be buried right next to the snortin' post in a big corral."

"Why?" Tyson asked.

"'Cause I want to hear them studs whistle when they bring the mare by."

"About all you're going to get bein' buried by the snortin' post is a helluva lot of horse piss." Kate laughed, and walked off into the shadows towards her sugan next to Wayne's.

"What do you make of this place, Tyson?" Leonardo asked.

"It's sure strange, just setting here in the middle of the barrens."

"It's because of the creek; there must be a fault line up at the head of the valley that breaks the water out," Frank said.

"Then it runs on east to that broken granite," Tyson said.

"And then goes underground again." Frank nodded.

"What's interestin'," Leonardo said, "is there's so much horse sign."

"I never noticed," Frank said.

"Me neither. Are you sure?" Tyson said.

"Might just be one lost horse in the whole lost valley, but I reckon I know a horse bun when I see it."

An owl called and they heard the soft whoosh of his wings, then the squeak of a mouse. Life and death in less than a minute.

Again they heard a rattle of rocks, followed by the hammering of hooves on bare rock, the nickering of nervous horses, then an explosive snorting and neighing.

"There's a stud out there wants your mare, Tyson," Leonardo murmured.

"He can't have her."

Tyson stood and tried to see outside the firelight.

"You got her hobbled?"

"No, she'll come if I whistle."

"Put hobbles on her front legs," Leonardo said,

getting up and going out into the edge of the fire-light where the mare stood like a statue, her neck raised, her head high, moving about, listening.

With Leonardo's help, Tyson slipped on the rawhide hobbles and retreated back to the fire.

"If she's horsin', she'll get bred, hobbles or not," Frank said.

"Yes, but he won't be ridin' her all through camp." Leonardo nodded.

"She's horsin'," Tyson said. "Been nervous all day."

"You goin' to be the proud owner of a hammer-headed mustang colt then," Frank said.

"She deserves better," Tyson said. "Suppose I stay with her all night?"

"They'll fool you," Leonardo said.

"Suppose I have my old .45 ready for the stud when he comes drivin'."

"It's too dark. Maybe you could kill him, maybe he'd kick your head off."

"I ain't afraid of him."

"Nobody's talking about bein' afraid," Leonardo said calmly. "Why not let it happen? She might throw you a colt that can't be beat."

"He'll have to earn it," Tyson said. "I'm goin' to tie my blanket over her butt."

Carrying the blanket out to the mare, he tried to tie it securely over her hind end. It wasn't as easy as he thought, and she was restive, nickering a come hither, and dancing.

"Reckon I'll sleep by the fire," Tyson said, putting his back to a tree.

In a few minutes young Tyson sat by the fire alone, listening to the others snore and murmur.

He could see the dun mare grazing off at the edge of the firelight, hopping awkwardly forward when she wanted to move.

As the fire died down to a core of glowing embers, Tyson's eyes slowly closed as if weighted with lead, and without knowing it, he drifted off into a vague dream.

Suddenly he heard the grunt and whistle of the wild stud tearing at the blanket on the mare's rump with his bared teeth.

Spellbound, not sure if he was dreaming or not, he saw the big blue roan with wide forehead and small nose rip the blanket aside.

The mare spraddled her hind legs, as the stud came at her, demanding that she break before him.

Her tail was raised and curled off to one side and the stud didn't hesitate. Rising on his hind legs, his huge red member cocked upward, he lunged forward and drove into the swollen vagina. Three, four, five, six times, he rocked back and forth on his powerful hind legs, his front knees bent, the hooves clipping the mare's shoulders, and then with a final exultant lunge, he bowed over her and seized her mane in his teeth, demanding more from the sweating, broken servant.

In a moment he slipped away along her near side, stood there a moment proud and mighty beside the bowed mare, then picked up his feet and trotted neatly away into the darkness.

=== 10 ===

SHIG RADIGUET WANTED A BIG MEAL, BUT HE had to be content with the boiled eggs and tortillas with cheese in the saloon.

A boy came in carrying a bucket full of tamales wrapped in a clean flour sack, and Shig bought half of them.

Piling them on the bar, he nodded to Bletcher, said, "Dig in," and started unwrapping the cornhusks.

"Not me," Bletcher said. "Mama could have laced the chili sauce with strychnine and you'd never taste it."

Bletcher cracked a hard-boiled egg, peeled it, and dipped it in a bowl of salt.

Shig Radiguet stared at the steaming tamale, which smelled like ambrosia, looked at the pale greenish-colored egg in Bletcher's grimy fingers, and thought about it.

"Should have made the kid eat one," Bletcher added, taking a bite out of the rubbery egg. "Then we'd know."

"Why the hell didn't you say so, then?" Shig growled, and threw the half-opened tamale at the wall.

The bartender backed unobstrusively out the back door.

"Why don't he come?" Shig asked for the sixth time that morning.

"Why should he come?" Bletcher asked, spitting crumbs of eggshell onto the bar. "He's taken his sixty thousand and rode off to El Paso, Juarez, and points south. If I was him, I'd never come back."

"You ain't him. You're just a cheap-jack skunk, but he's a fool. He believes in making things right."

"He believes in army payrolls." Bletcher chuckled, his eyes mean.

"He's got to come at me for killin' his greaser buddy. If he passes, they won't trust him anymore, and they'll give him to me just to prove it."

"I ain't no expert on Mexican brainpower, but I'll bet you money, marbles, or chalk they ain't going to give you nothing except a bullet in the back some dark night."

"It won't go that far. He'll come to me. Here. Right here. And it ought to be right soon." Shig Radiguet's blocky, stubbled face shone with the joy of anticipation.

"How you goin' to handle him?"

"Depends. If he starts in here, you head out the back door so he'll think you're gone, but you beat it around to the front. Take your boots off so he don't hear you. I'll talk him down some and find out where the payroll is. Then you come in from

156

the front and we've caught him in cross fire and he goes down fast."

"We split the payroll?"

"And the bounty on his head. That's substantial." Shig nodded, thinking Bletcher was even a bigger jackass than he looked. The main thing was to locate that payroll before the old man gave it away or lost it.

"How do you know he's even in the neighborhood?"

"He's within thirty miles of here right now," Shig said, looking out into the dusty street where a few rangy chickens scratched through the horse manure.

A hush lay over the small village. At the end of the street, a group of Mexicans dressed in black were gathered outside a whitewashed adobe chapel for Enrique's funeral.

Shig and Bletcher strode out onto the boardwalk and off to the left two doors to the combination jail and sheriff's office.

Inside, they found the sheriff, a small, wiry man wearing high-heeled boots and a black suit. Incongruously on top of a full head of straight black hair was perched a Chihuahua straw hat.

He was just buckling on his battered old Confederate Navy .44 Colt.

"Any word from the telegraph office?" Shig asked, towering over the button-sized Mexican.

"Nothing. What do you expect?"

"I'm hoping somebody's seen Carrol and reported it." Shig tried to be patient with the unsmiling Mexican.

The small sheriff thought he might tell the U.S. Marshal of the report his cousin had brought this morning of Don Wayne arriving in Agua Prieta last night, just to make him sweat, but he thought again that maybe the big man would sweat more if he knew nothing.

"Where you goin'?" Shig grabbed the sheriff by the lapels as he started out the door.

"No me chingues!" Sheriff Echevarria spoke in a high-pitched Yaqui dialect with such force that Shig released the coat and stepped back.

After a long, tense moment of staring at each other, Shig laughed and said, "Hell, I could break you into bread crumbs and feed you to the sparrows."

"I am the sheriff of this town and I'm the only reason you're alive right now."

"Bullshit!" Shig Radiguet blustered. "You're nothin' and this raggedy-assed town is nothin'."

"Excuse me, I'm going to the funeral of my uncle," the sheriff said coldly, and walked out the door, mounted his Spanish mule, and rode off toward the chapel.

"I don't think that sheriff cottons to us." Bletcher grinned. "Why didn't you just snap his neck?"

"We need him to hold the greasers down until Carrol rides in."

"Suppose he don't come?"

"Maybe I'll shoot a couple more of his buddies just to hurry him up," Radiguet growled.

As they walked back to the saloon, a few rocks came whistling over their heads, and bounced off the adobe wall. Across the street, down a goat run between the buildings, scooted three nearly naked boys, leather slingshots in their hands.

"Reckon it's about time for us to leave," Bletcher said, hustling in the door ahead of Radiguet.

"You scared of a few little kids?" Radiguet laughed.

"There ain't a white man in this town except us." Bletcher went behind the bar and found a bottle of Mexican brandy.

"Don't forget I wear this badge."

"I'm not going to spend another night here," Bletcher said. "It's a trap."

"You'll do what I tell you, Bletcher."

Bletcher said nothing, but studied the label on the brandy bottle while he considered exactly what he was here for.

Half of sixty thousand dollars was his reason, but weighed against fighting a whole town, it wouldn't pucker a hog's butt.

"My feelings is . . ." Bletcher said carefully, "we should find him before he finds us."

"Damn it, don't be so damned dumb! He's out there in the mountains, and no track to him. We have to bait him in."

159

"Sure enough, Shig, but when little kids are throwin' rocks, how long before the old soldiers turn up with their muskets?"

"I can wipe out this whole town with my Spencer," Radiguet said, nodding toward the repeater rifle standing in the corner. "And I've got enough ammunition to do it, too."

"Where is it?"

"In my saddlebags, over—"

"Ten to one they've taken our rigs and horses."

"How come you're always thinkin' the worst all the time?" Radiguet roared, his eyes hot, his right hand hovering over his six-gun. "If you can't think of something funny to say, keep your fat mouth shut."

"Sure, pardner, don't get excited. Let's just stroll over to the barn and check the horses."

The street was empty. Nothing stirred.

"Where is everybody?" Shig growled.

Bletcher was about to say the whole town was at the funeral when he thought better of it. Instead he silently shrugged his shoulders.

Turning left, they walked the half block to the makeshift livery stable.

The pole corral was empty, as well as the adobe stable. Nothing. Only a gray burro who seemed too old to move stood by the open gate, his eyes closed.

"The bastards!" Shig muttered, seeing how it was going. "They mean to fight us."

"Not if the sheriff is straight."

"You ever know a greaser straight with a gringo?" Shig growled, then stamped angrily back toward the saloon.

This time there were no rocks, but as the batwing doors closed behind them, an old shotgun from across the way fired and belched out a slow-going load of bent horseshoe nails, lead balls, and pebbles, doing no damage except to litter the boardwalk with the load.

"That's what you got to fight." Shig Radiguet grinned. "They don't even know how to load their damned old scattergun."

"The stage might bring in some soldiers that'd help keep law'n order," Bletcher said, pouring a glass of brandy.

"Keep thinkin' that way," Shig Radiguet said, "but we don't want too many soldiers stirrin' around our business. It's their payroll, remember."

With the funeral over, the people went to the restaurant down the block where they ate from a variety of delicious appetizers, pork from a pig that had been boiled in its own oil during the night, and pastries brought in by friends and relatives of Enrique's family from as far away as Agua Prieta.

Since everyone in Tres Cruces was related to Enrique, it meant the town was shut down, while in the shade of the ramada behind the restaurant, the men were drinking tequila, mezcal, aguardiente, and pulque.

Their spokesman, Chapo, had arrived with his

family in time for his brother's funeral, and quietly assumed the authority over the whole family.

True enough, their father, who was blind and a little odd in the head, held the title, which they all respected, but it was Chapo they looked to for leadership.

He was discovering that such a position wasn't without problems.

"We'll kill them in the night," the older men were murmuring, sorting out their plans by trying out their various ideas. There was no hurry. The children were watching the saloon. If the pair tried to make a break for the stage station, then there would be a fight *ya pronto*, but otherwise, let the flies buzz about and let us consider how this matter will find itself settled.

"Don Wayne asked that we wait," Chapo said quietly.

"He is not one of us. He hasn't the blood of the Echevarrias," the little sheriff said.

"But he has shared what he had with us without fail," an old man with stiff white hair said, and then knocked back a cup of mezcal.

"Why not let a gringo kill a gringo?" a burly grouch asked.

"Don Wayne is more than just a gringo," Chapo offered quietly.

"Muchos son los amigos y pocos los escogidos," said a young vaquero. "There are many friends, but not many of first choice."

"Ni todo dar, ni todo negar," said another older man smoking a cigarette made of a cornshuck and rough tobacco. "Don't give all or deny all."

Chapo knew they would sit around all day saying old adages and rhyming proverbs that meant very little, yet making it plain that they were present and available for whatever task.

"Mas vale a quien Dios ayuda, que quien mucho madruga," said a fat man whose shirt wouldn't button over his belly. "Better the help of God than to get up early."

"Aquel que al cielo escupe, a su cara se cae," murmured another Echevarria, dozing off. "He who spits in the sky will get it in the face."

"I prefer to wait for Don Wayne, if it's all right with everyone else," Chapo said into the hot, languorous afternoon.

There were murmurs of agreement and dissent. It didn't matter. Nothing would be done until it cooled off.

"Why should we ask our friend to kill this family's enemies?" a heavy-shouldered farmer responded. "That's what I don't like."

"Only that he asked."

"Then why didn't he come with us and do it?"

"That, I don't know," Chapo said. "He must have had a reason."

"A good reason is that one man against those two is a big risk," someone else said gently.

"Quien lengua ha, a Roma va," advised another

Echevarria from the table where he was pouring a tiny cup of tequila. "He who has a tongue, to Rome will go."

In that way, the afternoon passed without anyone losing his temper or raising his voice, for it made little difference if the pair now isolated in the saloon died today or tomorrow.

As the shadows slanted eastward, Shig Radiguet began to realize that his plan was not working. It should have been so simple. You raise some hell and shoot a friend of Carrol's to send out the challenge. If he was any kind of a man, he'd come charging and run smack into Radiguet lead. But he hadn't come, and probably wouldn't come in the dark. A man like Carrol liked to have things up and up and in broad daylight.

Shig had told the warden it would be a good idea to slow the outlaw down some, break his body and shake his nerve, but not kill him until they had the payroll.

Maybe it had broke him down too much. Maybe he couldn't answer a challenge. Maybe he couldn't find his nerve anymore.

Still, just two years ago, the old bastard had killed the Chamberlains even after they'd sprung their trap on him. Killed all three of 'em in less than a minute, picked up the saddlebag full of money, got on his horse, and rode off. Any man could do that had to have something extra.

Maybe it was a lie, one of them stories stretched

out by gossips, like Hickok shootin' all those McCanlesses. Hell, everybody knew he only kilt the one.

But Carrol had more than one of those yarns backin' his hand. Seemed like whenever someone picked on him, he'd let it go on longer than most men would, and then he'd say, back your play. There'd be some dead men and he'd mount up and ride off somewhere else.

"Maybe we burned his beans in the hotbox," Shig worried. "If he's broke down, we'll play hell findin' that payroll."

"Still, he's got the kid and the nauch. You can hide one, but you can't hide three." Bletcher smiled.

Tyson said nothing of the vision of the stallion bearing down on the mare. The ragged, stomped blanket told the story.

"Maybe you can get a good look at the damned keg-headed broomtail," Wayne said, leaning back against a pine tree, letting Kate bring him a breakfast of fried sowbelly and flapjacks.

"Mighty fine belly-packin' material," he said gratefully as Kate filled his coffee cup again. "I'll likely rest up here for the day, so's we can ride for Hermosillo tomorrow."

Tyson glanced at his father again. He didn't look to be in that bad a shape, but maybe that's the way it went when Father Time put his loop on you.

"I'd like to look the valley over some," Tyson murmured. "Don't look to be as bad as you think."

"You know blamed well that if them folks that calls themselves pioneers ain't found it and ruined it for everybody else, then it don't have no value," Wayne grumbled, and started on another stack of flapjacks.

"Mind if we ride along?" Frank asked, as Tyson left the campfire and caught the dun mare.

"Why should I mind?" Tyson asked sharply.

"Fine." Leonardo smiled, and in a few minutes the three riders were walking their horses down the south side of the valley.

"Lion sign," Frank said, leaning over his nervous horse's shoulder and looking at the ground. "Lots of it."

Farther along they came upon a rack of horse bones, old and weathered, the big leg bones cracked, gnawed, and scattered.

"Lions?" Tyson asked.

"No, wolves. There's his jawbone. He was a big old horse and the wolves cut him down."

They encountered deer that only moved aside, and a badger lumbering through the grass. A fox barked up in a small coulee, and overhead, eagles and hawks soared.

It took them till noon to reach the other end of the valley.

"Make it nine or ten miles." Frank scratched his chin judiciously.

"My thinking, too. And that's a big pasture."

Crossing over, they found where the creek bubbled up from an eroded granite throat at the base of a high up-and-down cliff, and then they crossed over to the north side and on the way discovered a primitive dam and a canal that carried the water off onto the flats.

"That's why there's so damned much grass." Frank nodded. "Indians worked out some irrigation."

"But where are they? Where's their houses?"

"Something wiped them out fast a long time back. Their tepees have rotted away. Likely there in the shelter of the cliff," Leonardo said.

"It don't seem right for a bunch of people to have a whole valley of grass and pine trees and water, then they just up and disappear," Tyson said.

"Likely they wanted to stay," Frank said laconically. "More lion sign."

"I make it jaguar," Leonardo said.

"Could be. I just never thought of jaguars this far north."

"We're not all that much north, that's what's strange," Leonardo said.

"Look!" Tyson said, catching sight of a herd of running horses, crossing the stream, fleeing from the riders.

"Boil me for a seahorse!" Frank said in awe.

"Jalisco! Look at the stud!"

Tyson had already recognized the big horse. He wasn't any keg-headed rat-tailed mustang, he was the biggest horse he'd ever seen, and with his swollen neck and high head emblazoned with a white star, he looked like an imaginary horse out of an old tale.

His blue color, the glowing blue roan hue, came from a rich blending of black, gray, white, and yellow, but his fetlocks were slightly darker than the silver blue of his withers.

His tail and mane were of that same ghostly blue color, floating lightly like picturesque waterfalls, or pale blue rain.

His hooves were generous, each one strong enough to carry his half ton striking the ground at forty miles an hour, and they pointed straight ahead as he stood or ran, leaving hoofprints parallel to each other. The dark pasterns were sloped at forty-five degrees from hoof to fetlock. His cannon bones were short and heavy, shielding the tendons from the brutal shock of going fast and far. His hooves were directly below his knees. His hind legs dropped almost straight down to his hocks. His shoulders were long and sloping, giving him an easy and powerful stride. He was deep in the chest, his ribs well sprung, providing for plenty of oxygen. His long withers indicated the spinal muscles of the long strider. His neck was not long nor short, but seemed to be in perfect proportion with the rest of his great conformation. His forehead was broad and open, his eyes large and clear amethyst, his ears attentive but hardly noticeable. His muscular hindquarters meant pure speed.

Following him were some thirty mares, colts, and fillies, all with the star imprinted on their foreheads and all roans.

"There ain't a runt in the whole cavvy," Frank said.

"I'd give my left *huevo* for any one of them," Leonardo said.

"But . . . but how?" Tyson was for once dazzled out of his grim cynicism.

"Lions, wolves, jaguars keep them runnin'. Yet there's so much grass, they don't suffer from hunger. If they don't get bigger, faster, and tougher, they'd soon be a rack of gnawed bones," Leonardo said quietly.

"That's the best-looking stud I ever saw in my whole life," Tyson said. "But I don't see why there aren't any jugheaded mustangs."

"Likely the Indians taken a herd of horses off some early Spaniards with pure stock. You can see the Arab in all of them with their little noses and wide heads. Likely they got the extra backbone, too," Frank said.

"Crossed onto another strain. English hunter, or Belgian draft brought into Spain by the French or English crusaders. Whatever it was, made a hell of a cross." Leonardo nodded.

"Could be they threw a sport like Justin Morgan or the Hambletonian," Frank suggested.

Off to one side, young stallions kept to the outside of the herd, and if one tried to mingle in with the mares, the blue roan would whirl and attack with his teeth bared, rising and striking with his forefeet, or whirling and letting his hind hoofs smack against the ribs of his son.

"But inbreeding ought to run 'em down," Tyson argued.

"Maybe if there was fewer of 'em and nothin' to eat, but look for yourself what you've got."

"What I've got?" Tyson repeated, confused by the revelation of fine running colors and fluid power.

"In a manner of speakin'," Frank added.

"Look at that colt over on the right. He's well started." Leonardo pointed out another blue roan stud, obviously not fully matured. "He's some salty. He'll be chasin' Papa down the trail one of these days."

"We could catch them, couldn't we?" Tyson asked, almost pleading.

"I ain't seen a horse I couldn't catch yet." Leonardo smiled. "But I reckon we're wastin' our time. Wayne wants to go south."

"And I'm feelin' so hungry," Frank chuckled, "my belly thinks my throat's cut."

"I wish . . ." Tyson said, still keeping his eyes concentrated on the horse herd, "I wish . . ."

"Like they say, if wishes was horses, beggars would ride." Frank laughed, and kneed his piebald off to the east.

Coming back into camp, Tyson was full of

enthusiasm, and yet in front of his dad, he was too shy to show it.

"Just mainly rocks and deadfall pines, I suppose," Wayne groaned. "Wouldn't support a runt sheep, would it?"

"You never rode this valley?" Tyson asked suspiciously.

"Like I said, it was just in and out in a hurry."

"Well, there's a herd of the best goddamn horses on the face of the earth just upstream a couple miles," Tyson said, trying to control his voice.

"Mustangs? Likely there'd be a few ratty crowbaits wearin' out the grass."

"Ask Leonardo," Tyson said.

"They're runners. Half barb, maybe half standardbred."

"Well, ain't that something!" Wayne slapped his hand on his knee. "Reckon we could round 'em up and sell 'em to the army?"

"No, Dad!" Tyson said angrily. "They're too good for the army, they're . . . they're . . ." His voice cracked and moisture came to his eyes as he finally choked it out, ". . . beautiful!"

"Wonder how they get through the winter?" Kate asked into the long silence.

"I notice how the mountains fit around here so as the valley gets a lot of southern sun. Likely in the winter it's kind of like an oven with the rocky walls holdin' the heat through the night," Wayne said.

Frank glanced quizzically and said, "I seen that, but I didn't match it with the winter sun."

"You mean it's warm in here in the winter?" Tyson almost whooped with joy.

"Likely is, except, of course, they's some winters badder'n others," Wayne said, "but I'm too old for building up a whole new ranch." Wayne shifted his legs and winced. "We got enough money to live in Mexico like kings, for the rest of my life at least."

"How come you're always thinking of yourself?" Tyson cried out. "Why can't you let me do the work? I ain't helpless!"

"Child, you're talkin' about more work than you can imagine."

"Well, maybe Uncle Frank and Leonardo could help some." Kate came to Tyson's rescue.

"Hell, there ain't even a school for fifty miles," Wayne held out.

"Kate's been a teacher. She can start her own school," Tyson said strongly.

"Likely you'd be out building log cabins and such and wouldn't want to learn."

"Dad." Tyson knelt in front of his father. "Them horses is racehorses. We can win any race in the world, but we can't do it if I'm dumb when we go to the big city."

"You sayin' you want to study some?"

"That ain't what I said. I said I got to study a bunch whether I want to or not, because anybody

172

knows there's more sharpers back East than fleas on a blind hound dog."

"Let me think on it some, son. Best be patient. Something bad may turn up. For all we know, somebody owns the whole shebang."

"Nobody's ever found this place since the Indians died, Dad," Tyson said, almost pleading.

"No hurry. I ain't saying yes, I ain't sayin' no. I'm saying we better wait until we get settled."

"What settled?"

"Well, they's a U.S. Marshal your ma set on my trail!" Wayne was so close to comin' out with a big belly laugh, he had to make a joke to let himself bust it out.

"He'd never find us in here," Kate said, smiling, knowing he was teasing, and feeling the happiness he was trying so hard to hide.

"Sure, but sometime we have to go out and race the horses; we can't live like coyotes forever on the run."

"I reckon Leonardo and me can handle that marshal whilst you're restin' up," Frank said.

"You boys likely to make this old man cuss talking so. That marshal ain't after you, he's after me. When I can't kill my own snakes, then you can talk bad to me like that."

Frank almost hung his head in shame, he was so embarrassed.

"I just meant . . ." he said.

"Frank, I know what you meant, that's the worst

of it, so I'm holdin' my temper because you meant it good-hearted, but I've learned in a few short years that them good-hearted fellers can sap a man's strength more'n any hotbox the law ever figured out to torture helpless men with."

"I'm sorry, Wayne," Frank said, dead serious, "it's your play."

Kate watched and listened, and suddenly stood up, put her hands on her hips, and yelled, "What the hell are you jaybirds jabbering about? We're all talking about living, and we sure as hell won't let you go downtown and get yourself killed by an oversized turd wearin' a badge! Hear me! Now, I won't listen to any more of this he-man talk. I'll go kill him myself before you can find your ass, Wayne. I mean it."

She was crying now, shaking with anger and worry.

"So now, little sweetheart," Wayne said softly, "I can see now what I couldn't see before. Whatever we do in the way of life or death, we better do it together."

"You're lyin'!" she howled. "I know you're lyin'!"

"No, no more, girl. I used to lie like that and I beg your forgiveness for it, but now that I'm gettin' old, I've seen the light."

"Wayne, you devil, don't sweet-talk me!" She shook her finger angrily at him.

"Are we riding to Mexico?" Tyson put in.

"Soon as I'm able, but you can look over the ground some more. Hell, the whole thing is probably a breedin' place for giant running rattlesnakes," Wayne said, seriously.

"I want to catch that young stud," Tyson said, as if talking to himself.

"Now, Wayne," Kate put in, trying to see into his gray cat eyes, "I don't know the game, but you better not trick me."

"I'm so puny, I can't hardly lick my upper lip." Wayne smiled. "I suppose if a poor bag of bones like me asked for a bowl of stew, I'd hear oratory on into the night."

"Oh, hell," she said, grabbing up some pine needles to get the fire going, "I forgot all about dinnertime just trying to keep you alive."

She broke dead pine branches over her knee and built up the fire, then lifted the iron kettle over to the rocks.

"Things are happening too fast for me to keep track of," Kate said, putting tortillas on the lid of the kettle to warm.

"You mean you're about to settle down?" Wayne asked, his eyes closed, dozing.

= 11 =

I JUST DON'T SEE WHY HE DON'T WANT TO settle down right here," Tyson said to the broadshouldered Frank. As the three let their horses drink, big rainbow trout zigzagged away from them.

"Maybe he isn't done roaming," Leonardo said, thinking they were all getting a little too old for sleeping on the hard ground in any kind of weather, always with the idea that somewhere on their back trail was a lawman anxious as hell to hang you.

Most anyone could see, now that the telegraph was in place and people were learning more and more how to use it, the owl-hooter on a horse was all but finished.

Sometimes they'd talk around a little fire about how to win against the wire, but in the end it always came down to it that a man on a good horse could ride maybe forty miles in a day, and the telegraph could be passing on your description across that same forty miles in less than a minute. That meant a posse on fresh horses would be coming out to meet you before you hardly even got into the saddle.

There was still some room up toward Canada, in Wyoming, Montana, and Idaho, but anybody could see how the net was closing on the long riders.

Prudent men were taking up ground and looking at a predictable future where they'd work, sleep, and eat without worrying about the end coming, but how many of the old-time owl-hooters could be called prudent men?

Still, something had to give, and it was the owl-hooters who'd be hung from the telegraph poles if they didn't change.

This time they stayed in the middle of the valley, riding close to the stream. Midway they came to a beaver dam which spread the stream into a fan of smaller rivulets, creating a bog that someday would firm up and make a birch and poplar woodland.

Even as they approached, Tyson heard the loud crack of a beaver tail on the water, and when they came upon the pond itself, he saw only gnawed trees fallen crosswise to the stream.

"Old buck beaver heard us coming." Frank smiled.

Again they sat back in their saddles and surveyed the valley ahead. High up, the rimrocks were naked granite scarps too steep to climb, but the belt of pines on the side slopes were in a completely natural state, from big, gnarly granddaddies, lightning-blasted, down to seedlings growing in open spaces left by others that had simply fallen from old age.

"Man could snake logs for a cabin down from there in less'n a week," Frank said.

"You ready for blisters off an ax handle?" Leonardo asked seriously.

"No. I'm not," Frank said after thinking it over, "but if I had to, I would."

Tyson said nothing, but he too saw the potential ranchstead like a dream.

Flashing through the lower trees, the colorful horse herd came dashing, spooked by their presence or perhaps by a big cat.

In shades of gray, from blue to almost white, they came dashing, manes in the wind, heads high, the big-shouldered stud leading the way. Seeing the three riders, he slowed to a quick trot, his eyes flashing, snorting and whistling.

Neither of the geldings nor Tyson's mare was interested.

Off on the flank, the long-legged younger stud led his own group of young stallions, clearly in charge of them.

"I'd like to catch that one," Tyson said.

"Much horse," commented Frank.

"Couldn't we do it?" Tyson insisted.

"Depends." Leonardo took his braided rawhide riata from his saddle fork, and shook out a loop.

Glancing at Frank, Leonardo said, "Game?"

"Hell, yes, I'm just wondering what we'll do with him after we catch him," Frank said, undoing his own hemp lasso.

"Think you could rope him if we push him to you?" Leonardo asked Tyson quietly.

"I'd like a try," Tyson replied, undoing his own lasso, a well-stretched sisal he'd been given by Wayne. "The mare is a good roper."

He'd roped a few gateposts and the mare a few times, but she was standing still and holding her head up for him, so while he thought he was as good a roper as anyone else, Leonardo at least thought otherwise.

"Listen, Tyson, my son," Leonardo cautioned

him, "you do not tie your lass to the horn. Understand? If your loop goes over his neck, dally twice around the horn, keeping your thumb out of the way or you will lose it. Then once he starts to fall, give him just enough slack to break his fall and let him hit the ground like a feather."

"Why be so danged complicated?" Tyson flushed angrily, knowing he couldn't do all those things in one motion.

"A horse with a broken bone is a dead horse," Leonardo said as sternly as a schoolteacher. "Do you want me to catch him for you?"

"Hell, no, he's my horse," Tyson said.

"Very well," Leonardo said. "If you say so. But remember, if you don't slip your dally, something must give."

"That's a strong colt," Frank said, looking over the terrain ahead where the wild horses had bunched, their heads up, their small ears pointing at the three riders.

"I don't think we can catch him," Leonardo said, looking at Frank, "but we can head him."

Frank nodded.

"You, my young vaquero, you station yourself over there where the pine trees start to grow. You must be running at the same time as he comes by you. You'll only get the one chance."

"I don't know why you're always treating me like a kid," Tyson snapped nervously. "If you can bring him near me, I'll rope him."

"I'm trusting you," Leonardo said, and kneed his sorrel gelding off to the left so that he could make a gradual circle and come in behind the horse herd. Frank in turn went to the right as Tyson rode off to the edge of the valley where the forest would hold back a hard-running horse.

The boss stud whistled and whirled about, trying to watch Leonardo and Frank at the same time.

He snorted and wheeled, leading his band off toward Frank, then, turning, came back toward Leonardo.

The group of younger stallions mingled with the rest of the herd, but Leonardo had his eyes on the young stud, and kept his sorrel working towards him, until the sorrel had the target fixed in his mind.

The stud roared off to the right, cutting across in front of Leonardo, who kneed his sorrel quickly forward to head off the young stallion.

Frank came in from the left, and in less than a minute they had cut the young stud free from the main herd and were moving him down the valley at a gallop.

Each time he tried to swing around one of the riders, the rider would ask a little extra from his mount and cut him off, forcing him to waste his strength moving one way and then the other. Down near the timber line, young Tyson kneed the mare into an easy canter.

The young roan wasn't paying attention to the

cantering horse and rider off to his left, rather he was picking up the pace, wanting very much to get back with his friends and family.

That stud can run a mile in a minute right now with a hundred twenty pounds on his back to boot, Leonardo thought, kicking his sorrel into an all-out gallop, keeping the roan headed down valley.

In a moment they were bearing down on young Tyson.

"Go get him, boy!" Leonardo yelled, and asked his sorrel for a final burst of speed as the roan shied away from Tyson, who had the mare flying, his loop clutched in his right hand.

The stud turned away from Leonardo and put his belly to the grass as he charged ahead.

He was too fast, but Tyson tried. Swinging the lass rope over his head once, he cast the loop and made a fair catch, the rope slipping well down the stud's extended neck.

Now Tyson jerked the reins, sat back, and with his left hand, meant to make the turns around the saddle horn so that he could snub down the stud.

The mare sat down on her heels and skidded to a stop.

But the stud was running too fast, hurtling like a lightning bolt with the force of a freight train, not giving Tyson that split second to make his dally.

The rope burned through his hand, and instead of releasing it, he stubbornly hung on to it with all his might.

181

The mare was stopped and set, the stud still going at a full gallop, and in an instant Tyson was flying through the air like a fish on the end of a line.

As he crashed to the ground, he blacked out. The shock opened his hands and the rope went on its way.

He lay still, his arms extended, his face hidden in the grass. The mare stood calmly, waiting.

Leonardo and Frank arrived at the same time, and leaping from their blowing horses, knelt beside the crumpled youth.

Leonardo put his ear to Tyson's back, and after a moment said quietly, "He lives."

Frank checked the boy's legs first for a break, and shook his head. "Thank God for the grass," he muttered.

Between the two of them, they gently rolled the boy over on his back. His arms and legs flopped loosely.

There was a rising knob on Tyson's left temple, and Leonardo listened to his breathing.

"Not so good," he said, frowning, and ran his fingers over Tyson's ribs.

"Couple bent ribs," he said.

"Damn it," Frank said. "Wayne'll be some displeased."

"Didn't he say he was a roper? Maybe next time he'll think twice."

"That's a hard way to learn a little lesson," Frank

said, as Tyson opened his eyes and looked straight up at the sky.

"You in there?" Frank growled, hiding his relief.

"I'm fit. Let me get my breath," Tyson said slowly as his mind sorted out his aches and pains, determining what was most serious. "Lost him," Tyson said.

"A good thing, too." Leonardo smiled. "He'll shake loose your lass rope later on."

"I want to ride him," Tyson said stubbornly, and tried to sit up. The pain in his chest hit him, and he groaned, and eased back onto the grass.

"Cracked a couple ribs," Leonardo said. "Lucky that's all. If your spurs had tangled in your riggin', God knows what you'd look like."

"Look about ten foot long." Frank grinned. "Fit you through a keyhole."

Opening Tyson's shirt, they could see the bruise on his right side, and with nothing else to use, they took off their wide belts and, with the scanty padding of their bandannas, cinched up the belts on the lower chest so that he couldn't damage himself too much riding back to camp.

"This won't be no Sunday school picnic," blocky Frank said gently, "but you got to do it anyways."

When they lifted him into his saddle, Tyson's face went greenish pale, his eyes shut hard, and his teeth locked together.

After a minute he took a little breath and said softly, "Let's ride."

"No hurry," Leonardo said, coming close alongside in case Tyson fainted.

"I'll make it," Tyson gritted.

Leonardo looked sidewise at Frank and nodded, a faint smile on his lips.

At camp they helped Tyson down off the mare and laid him on a blanket, while Kate fussed over him.

After they'd explained the bare-bones story, Frank and Leonardo went off to take care of the horses, while Wayne leaned back against the pine tree, saying, "It happens sometimes."

"Maybe, but I bragged myself right into turning the outhouse over and fallin' in," Tyson said grimly.

"It's just a way of learning, Tyson," Kate said, removing the belts; after cutting off a six-inch strip of the blanket with her belt knife, she commenced wrapping him up again.

"I'm about ready to give up on learnin'," Tyson said, painfully.

"Take your time," Wayne said. "Soon as you're healed up some, we'll go down to Mexico and buy us a regular hacienda. Plenty good horses down there, already broke, don't worry."

"Dang it, Dad," Tyson said, trying to speak slowly, "what's the all-fired hurry to get somewhere else?"

"Wasn't it you wanted to see the world?" Wayne asked. "What do you want?"

"I want to ride that young stud," Tyson said. "I'm going to build a trap corral up there out of logs, run him in there, and gentle him down."

"Fine, son. Mexico can wait. Right, Kate?"

"I'm just the cook," she said, still not trusting Wayne's smooth voice.

When Leonardo and Frank returned to the camp, Wayne sat up and asked, "Seen enough?"

"Pretty little valley from head to toe," Frank said.

"Them horses is worth so much money, I can't guess the number," Leonardo said.

"They look pretty in here on their own grass, but put 'em in an auctioneer's corral and they'll look like any other jughead cayuse," Wayne said.

"Beggin' your pardon, but these roans are a hand taller than any riding horse I ever saw," Leonardo said. "The boss stud, he's two hands taller."

"That's eight inches," Tyson murmured.

"Well, maybe they'd make good draft animals, I ain't saying they're hopeless mustangs. Cross 'em on a Clydesdale maybe, they might pull a beer wagon."

"Dad, you're plumb loco," Tyson said angrily, and as the pain bit into his lung, he shut his eyes and set his jaw again.

Without changing expression, Wayne looked dourly at Leonardo and winked his left eye. "It comes with age, son," he said. "Sometimes a man in his prime just loses his sand and forgets everything he ever learned."

185

Leonardo looked at the ground and shook his head slowly.

"Dad, we didn't find no running giant rattlesnakes anywhere today."

"No sign?"

"I seen a lion been kicked to death," Frank said.

"And I noticed one of the young fillies had some claw marks on her butt," Leonardo added.

"It's wild out here. Likely the Apaches would be here in a minute iffen they knew there was a herd of mustangs to be had."

"I thought you and old Cochise was buddies," Tyson said, prodding.

"Well, maybe I mentioned we was acquainted, but just because we cut our wrists and mixed our blood don't mean he'd turn down a chance at that horse herd you think is so fancy."

This time, Wayne winked at Frank, whose solid brick face froze in shock.

Dusk was coming down on the valley, sky-lighting the western peaks that stood like jagged teeth hungering for the coming stars.

"Change of fare tonight," Kate smiled, and went to the stream, returning with a string of gutted trout, all between four and five pounds.

"You catch them?" Tyson asked.

Putting a pot of beans and a skillet with bacon grease on to warm, she rolled the big fish in cornmeal and nodded at Wayne. "No. The old-timer hobbled over to the creek, took his boots off, waded out in there, and started throwing fish out on the bank like he was harvesting corn."

"We have a saying that rhymes." Leonardo grinned. *"Manos duchas, comen truchas."*

"What does that mean?" Tyson asked suspiciously.

"Quick hands, eat trout." Leonardo chuckled.

"Well, I'm glad to know that the ailing old-timer still has the fastest hands this side of the Big Muddy," Frank said stolidly.

"But nobody can catch a trout with his hands," Tyson protested. "It's just another yarn! I'll bet you threw a bomb of black powder in the creek."

"Sometime when you feel like it," Wayne said softly, "we'll do it together. I didn't ever know my pa, so I had to learn from a Cheyenne Indian, but I learned."

"Hush now, both of you," Kate said. "I seen him do it, Tyson. That's all there is to it."

"My teeth been getting some concerned whether they could go on with that jerky without some rest," Frank said, and let Kate fill his tin plate.

"You know, if a man was ever to settle a kind of a closed-in place like this," Wayne said conversationally, "railroader told me one time up somewhere in Idaho or someplace, my memory's failed me, the . . ."

"What was it, Dad?" Tyson tried to jog the old man back on track again.

"Something about land, wasn't it . . . ?"

"Yes, settling a valley," Tyson came back angrily.

"I recollect he said, the way to do it was to put a section in each one of your family's names. Each section is a square mile."

"Makes sense," Frank said. "But this valley is ten miles long at least."

"He said you leapfrog 'em. You get a section on the lower end and another on the head of the water, then you leapfrog 'em down your valley so's it's all yours whether anybody likes it or not."

"There's five of us," Tyson said quickly.

"I reckon if there was some wives and children, you might come up with ten someday," Wayne chuckled. "Now, what was I talking about?"

"Land," Tyson said.

"That's it. Land in Mexico. You can buy a whole Spanish land grant that takes up half the state of Nuevo Leon for sixty thousand dollars, and that includes big houses, horses, cows, goats, and about ten thousand Indians too."

"You mean you got to feed ten thousand Indians!" Tyson yelped.

"Well, everybody's got to eat," Wayne said mournfully.

Kate stared at him a moment, shook her head as if she had a mosquito in her ear, and went back to eating the tasty trout.

Night came down while the last light of day illumined the jagged peaks above them. Somewhere up there eagles nested, Wayne thought, and lions prowled and bears denned.

"I don't think I ever felt so content in my whole life as right now," he murmured, lighting up his pipe and viewing the orange-lighted rimrock. "We're safe here unless there's a flood or an earthquake."

"Well, then," Tyson said excitedly, "why don't we stay!"

"There's lots of things to consider. It don't do to just jump like a bullfrog in a swamp."

"Well, dang it, Dad, what is it?" Tyson asked, angry again.

"I'm worried some," Wayne said quietly, "as to whether you trust my judgment."

Tyson remained silent. He'd learned enough not to say what was in his mind, which was just what his dad feared. He didn't trust his dad's judgment for sour apples, and he just wished he'd go away and let him make his own ranch right here. But he couldn't say such a thing out in the open. There'd be a fight for sure.

Tyson wasn't concerned about who would win such a battle, he just didn't want the battle to even happen.

Looking up at the sawtooth mountains turning slowly reddish black, he wondered why. It wasn't that he was afraid of losing. He had a wagonload of confidence in his quickness and his strength and his youthfulness to master the failing old man, he just somehow wanted an expression of respect, something you couldn't ever get from such a fight. All you could get from that was that one of them would have to leave.

And much as he chafed against his dad's lead rope, he wanted something different than just busting it in two.

Danged, though, if he'd go to Mexico and leave Cache Valley! They'd have to drag him feet-first hollerin' all the way!

"You feelin' any better, Wayne?" Kate asked seriously.

"Not much worse, I reckon, thanks to you, but if you folks don't mind, I'm goin' to stretch out a while."

With that, he limped out of the firelight, found his bedroll, and collapsed like a coldcocked steer.

"You all right?" She hurried to his side.

"I don't know, girl, I just don't know," he sighed.

"What? What's on your mind?"

"I guess you can take care of things." He spoke in a low voice.

"What do you mean? Where you goin'?"

"Well, we all have to think of that speck of time where you just turn into a memory," Wayne teased.

"I'm going to send you to a veterinarian!" Kate exclaimed, and kissed him smack on the mouth.

"I wish I knew why that boy disrespects me so," he said in a whisper.

"He's just at that stage. He's feelin' studdy and all he's got to go against is you."

"But why not Frank, say, or Leonardo?"

" 'Cause they don't mean so much to him. He's got to find out how much sand he draws himself, and he does that by measuring against you."

"But I've run out of sand," Wayne said.

"Not likely. Once he finds out you're for real, he's going to have to fish or cut bait. He gets over that fence, he'll be man enough to talk to you level."

"They say a man that straddles a fence too long gets a sore crotch," Wayne said softly, dropping off to sleep.

Coming back into the firelight, she glared around at the three of them, and said tiredly, "I just don't know what's goin' on."

"I ain't goin' to Mexico," Tyson said firmly.

"Don't tell me, tell your dad. It's about time you started standin' up on your own two feet."

Tyson stared at her as if she'd just cut him with a quirt. "Yes'm," he mumbled, and crawled off to his blankets, wondering where she'd got the urge to treat him so.

From the old man, of course. They were over there in the dark runnin' him down right now.

Kate crept into her own blankets beside the sleeping Wayne and thought her whole world was crashing as he seemed to fail more each day. That goddamned hotbox in the Yuma pen had started

191

him downhill. They'd been nicer to have just put him against an adobe wall and shot him down.

She'd had a dog once, a water spaniel pup, and he was such a gay, happy little dog, brave enough to hunt bears, but then after about eight years, he'd changed. Lay around a lot, got tangles in his coat, and his eyes sunk in and turned red. Started losing teeth, and she'd fed him everything mashed up, but he didn't get better. His coat was so bad, but he wouldn't let her comb at the snarls because his skin was so sensitive, and then finally he lost all the controls, and laid his head on his paws and looked miserable.

Soon as her daddy noticed it, he led the old dog off behind the barn, and when she heard the shot, she thought, thank Heaven.

She didn't ever want Wayne to go down that way. She'd rather he faced a man with a gun and took the meaning of life very quickly smack between the eyes.

While off to one side, Leonardo had his head cradled in his saddle thinking it was about time to head out. He didn't want to get in any fracas between the boy and his dad, especially when the old man was failing.

Yet why had old Wayne winked at him? Maybe he'd imagined it, hoping it was all a joke after all. Maybe he'd just been wishing Wayne would let him know that none of this was serious, but hell, it was plenty serious.

"Ni modo." No answer.

Across the flat, so as not to disturb the rest of them, Frank McCloud slept heavily, snoring like a stop-and-start buzz saw with a peanut whistle in between.

The valley floor turned to white gold as the moon rose, and the plaintive weeping of a lion drifted down from its rocky pulpit.

Slowly, almost as slowly as the moon moved over the rimrock, Wayne eased out of his blankets, found his boots and hat, and crawled off toward the horses in the shadows.

12

THE FAILING LIGHT TURNED FROM A YELLOW to an orange haze that filled the inert air between the adobes on the main street of Tres Cruces. Doors were closed and windows shuttered, except at the saloon, where Shig Radiguet and Bletcher had taken over.

Down the street behind the restaurant, the people were gathered under the large brush ramada.

Behind that ramada was an unplanned dog run, and on back were scattered three or four more adobe houses.

The men had eaten, drunk, discussed their problems, and wisely taken a nap in the hottest part of the day. But as soon as the sun tilted over into the west and softened its rays, they awakened, and went off to stand around a broken-down adobe that smelled strongly of urine.

A few of them dunked their heads in the water trough and slicked back their hair.

Each one carried his machete in a leather sheath attached to his belt, but there were no revolvers except that of the sheriff. Chapo had brought his ancient Damascus twist shotgun, which matched the one his brother had tried to use on Shig. For that reason they had little confidence in their ability to shoot the two gringos.

Still, if they could not fight face-to-face with the gunmen, they could starve them to death. They had secured the horses; where could the gringos go?

As soon as the food in the saloon was gone, the gringos would have to come out. When that happened, God would find the proper solution.

They could wait. They had been waiting for centuries. *Así es la vida.* So is life.

No one expected the fiery little sheriff to single-handedly attack the gunslingers armed with new revolvers and repeating rifles. Of course, if anyone were to do anything, then he should do it.

And as the men and women went into the back of the restaurant for coffee and pastry, *Dios* contrived to send a small, furry puppy dog out into the main street. A brave and happy little dog, he pranced along with his tail curved over his back and his head up, observing all the strange things he had never seen before.

He barked at a rooster scratching in the dirt, he nosed through a pile of horse droppings, he chased a scrap of paper touched by the occasional breeze, all the while advancing toward the saloon. A calico house cat crossing the street excited him until she turned and cuffed him with unsheathed claws, hissed, and backed away, spitting hatred. On beyond, an old bony hound lay in the middle of the street in a depression he had excavated an hour earlier in front of the saloon.

Wagging his tail, the pup trotted forward to make friends with possibly his father, certainly his uncle, when a small, barefooted boy, wearing a pair of hand-me-down shorts, wandered out into the street and saw his puppy straying off.

"Cachorro!" he called, but the puppy didn't turn, and the boy hadn't named him yet, so that he didn't know he belonged to somebody.

"Cachorro!" the boy called, and trotted bow-legged after him.

The puppy had visiting his kin on his mind, and paid no attention to his young master, who was gaining on him, when suddenly there was a howl from the restaurant as Maria looked out the door and saw her little brother running toward the saloon.

"Chano!" she cried out, and the boy listened to her about as much as the pup listened to him. The boy's name was Feliciano and he was used to being called Chano, yet it didn't seem as important as bringing his dog back home.

"Chano!" Maria called.

Then her heavyset mother screamed, "Chano!"

By then he had caught the pup and was looking up at a huge man standing in the doorway of the saloon.

"Chano!" Maria yelled again, as the hue and cry went through the whole restaurant and men and women realized the little boy was in danger.

Not waiting, Maria, dressed now in shirt and overalls that her older brother had loaned her to replace the black frock she'd worn at the funeral, ran swift as a deer out into the street, grabbed the boy, and started to run back, but the big man moved out with deceptive speed and grabbed her by the arm.

She released the boy, yelling, *"A la casa!"* and struggled to free herself from the big man's massive hand.

At this time the brave little sheriff had to do what he had to do. Bursting out the door, he was drawing his old .45 when Bletcher stepped out from the saloon with his own .45 already in his hand, and, taking his time, shot the sheriff through the head so that he collapsed to the ground as if all his tendons and ligaments had suddenly been severed, leaving only a small slab of bones and flesh to fall.

Maria was hurled into the saloon as the little boy was gathered into his mother's arms. As the door slammed, Shig pulled his own Colt and fired three shots just for the fun of it at the door made of piñon slabs, which were hard enough to stop the bullets.

The sheriff lay exactly as he'd fallen, his old six-shooter lost in the dust.

"Hear me, you bastards!" Shig yelled. "You want this girl back, you better bring our horses first, and then you better get word to that Wayne Carrol to bring in the money. You hear me?"

No one answered. Shig didn't care. They could play dumb, but he had the girl, and after she screamed a couple times, they'd smarten up some.

He was still puzzled that Carrol hadn't turned up by now. He'd waited all day, holding himself together, only nipping on the brandy, ready for the killing, but the old man hadn't come.

For sure he wasn't over there with the Mexes. He would have been ahead of that runt of a sheriff.

Bletcher had lighted the hanging oil lamps, keeping an eye on Maria crouched in a corner, her eyes rolling white with fear.

"Good move, Shig," Bletcher said. "The little hellcat is just what we needed."

"Next time you shoot a man," Shig said, "shoot him in the belly so he knows it. That dumb sheriff never even felt nothin'."

"But he didn't shoot back neither." Bletcher grinned.

"Let's tie that little bitch and lock her up some-where."

"What are we savin' her for?" Bletcher replied stubbornly. "I want a go at her."

"Settle yourself, Bletcher. She's mine, when I want her, and you got nothin' to say about it."

"Bullshit!"

"It ain't bullshit, mister." Shig's fingers wrapped around the walnut butt of his .45. "You take it like I lay it out. She's mine. Maybe when I'm done with her, I'll let you plug her, but not till she's broke by me."

Bletcher looked at the small girl in overalls and shirt and then at Shig, and shook his head. "Hell, she looks more like a boy. You're welcome to break her if you like that kind."

"Watch yourself, Bletcher. I'm not to be hurried," Shig said, unbending. "Find some twine and tie her hands."

She fought them as best she could, biting and scratching until she had her teeth in the web of flesh between Shig's left thumb and fingers, and with his balled-up right fist, he swung an overhand right at the side of her head, and knocked her flat.

"I'll tame the son of a bitch soon enough," Shig growled. "I'll sell her to the miners up in Creede for fifty cents a crack."

"After I get my twenty dollars' worth for nothing," Bletcher added with an oily smile.

They dragged her into a storeroom at the side of the bar and pegged the door shut.

Peering out the back door, Shig looked to see

if the horses had been brought, but he saw nothing and heard nothing.

"Best barricade for the night," he growled, and shoved a table sideways against the front door, and backed it with two oak barrels. The back door received the same treatment. "I don't want nobody sneakin' up on us."

"It's going to be a long night." Bletcher nodded.

Again Shig went to the front door and yelled out into the street, "Listen to me, you bastards! I want our horses. Right now."

"Maria?" a man's voice came out of the darkness.

"You'll get her back when the horses are at the back door, and your goddamn Don Wayne Carrol brings in a boxful of money."

"Don Wayne, he's no here."

"He better be here, and damned soon," Shig roared, and stepped back toward the bar where Bletcher was pouring a drink.

"Think they'll do it?" Bletcher asked, his bearded features sagging from tiredness.

"They goddamn better or I'll stick a red-hot poker up that chili pepper's notch so you can hear her scream clear to Yuma and then some."

A few minutes later, Shig heard horse hooves in the backyard and peeked around the corner of the door to see the two horses saddled, their bridle reins tethered to a mesquite post.

"That's more like it," he growled. "Now we get

that old bastard in here with the payroll, and we'll be busier than a one-legged cowboy at an ass kickin'."

"We going to have to kill the old man?" Bletcher asked.

"We sure as hell don't want him doggin' us down forevermore." Shig nodded absently. He felt tired and mean. It was the waiting. He never liked to wait on anybody. "If I'd got the money off him when I had him in the mountains, I'd killed him then."

"How'd you catch him?"

"He was laying behind his horse and I creased his head with my .44-40. He was out cold, damned near dead as his horse, but he didn't have the money. So I hauled him off to Yuma."

"Tough old jaspar," Bletcher yawned.

"Keep an eye on those doors," Shig muttered, closing his eyes. "I need some shut-eye."

"I'll take care of everything, Shig," Bletcher said softly.

Waiting until the big man was breathing heavily, Bletcher slowly took his boots off, and stood in his bare feet.

He really wanted to shoot Shig Radiguet at that moment because it would have been so easy, but he reasoned that without Shig, he'd have a hard time talking the money out of Wayne Carrol, and also just getting away from the goddamn greasers was beginning to look like a problem.

He tiptoed through the dim light to the back of the room, and picking up a stinking towel off the bar, unpegged the hasp on the storeroom door.

Maria looked up at him, her eyes rolling white, her teeth bared, but she didn't scream.

Overcome by old Adam's he-goat lust, he shoved the bar towel over her mouth with his left hand and tried to unhook the straps on the overalls with the other, which in his haste couldn't happen fast enough.

Holding her squirming body down by the weight of his own, he finally got one of the wire hooks free, but with her hands tied behind her back, he couldn't slip the other one loose, and as he tried to use his left hand, the towel slipped away.

Her scream was released like a puff of steam through a train whistle for just a moment, and then he was struggling to get the strap off her shoulder again. This time it slipped enough so that he could pull the garment down, but in his savage fury and haste, all he could encounter was still more crumpled clothing.

"What the hell?" Shig's voice filled the storeroom.

Bletcher froze. His heart stopped a beat, as his mind raced to return to normal.

Bletcher backed away from the girl on his knees. "I told you . . ."

"Don't worry, Shig, I don't want her. She's just as good as new."

Clear of the girl now, he rose and turned. He couldn't draw because he didn't know if Shig had him under the gun.

Sure enough, Shig was just a hundredth of a second from blowing his backbone out his belly.

"Don't get riled, I was just playing." Bletcher tried to chuckle. "Have to pass the time somehow."

"I won't tell you again," Shig Radiguet said, holstering the .45 and thinking just as soon as he had the money, he would shoot the son of a bitch about as low as you can shoot anybody and let him die slow or learn crocheting.

"I'd be afraid to get close to her again. As soon as you come down, she'd tear your throat out with her teeth."

"The way you do that is when you come down, you hit her a good lick with a six-gun barrel."

"What is it, halfway to daybreak?" Bletcher asked.

"More'n that. I'd order some coffee and breakfast, if I thought the sons a bitches wouldn't poison us."

"Maria can eat with us." Bletcher grinned, and Shig Radiguet nodded agreeably.

"You there!" Shig yelled from the barricaded front door. "We want coffee and ham and eggs and tortillas. Breakfast. Understand?"

"Maria?"

"She's going to eat with us. You poison us, you poison her, understand?"

"Sí, señor."

"And hurry it up, goddamn it."

In a few minutes platters of food arrived on top of the barrels as if by magic from the fading darkness, and Shig and Bletcher carried them to the bar.

"Go ahead," Shig said.

"In a minute, soon as I get my boots on," Bletcher said.

"I said go ahead, goddamn you," Shig growled, his hand again on the butt of his six-gun.

Bletcher looked carefully at the eggs staring up at him from steaming chili sauce with tomatoes and green pepper slivers floating about.

"They spiced it so much, you couldn't taste strychnine," Bletcher said.

"They won't poison us as long as we got Maria."

Bletcher turned his attention to a hot corn tortilla. He knew there could be nothing in it except corn that had been soaked in limewater and ground to flour. Maybe a little salt, but except for the water necessary to make the dough, there should be nothing else.

He bit off the edge of the tortilla, tasted it, ready to spit it out if it was bitter.

But it was as bland as any other tortilla.

"It's all right," he said, dipping the tortilla into the yolk of the egg. "Not bad."

Satisfied, Shig ate hungrily, and as the first pink of dawn showed on the eastern skyline, Shig Radiguet threw the platters out the front door into the street.

"Hear me!" he yelled. "I want Carrol. Send somebody after him. I want the money."

"Why don't you come out and get it?" came the raspy voice of Wayne Carrol.

Shig Radiguet ducked back instinctively even as his mind told him that his man had finally arrived.

"Is it him?" Bletcher stepped forward, his six-gun in his hand.

"It's him," Radiguet said. "Now we've got to catch him in a cross fire."

"Are you coming out, you yellow-striped polecat?" the raspy voice called.

"Where you been, old man?" Shig yelled back to cover his planning.

"He don't know where you are. Now, get up on the roof with the Spencer, and whilst he's looking at me, shoot the shit out of him."

"Why is he looking at you?"

"I'm going to be calling him."

"How will that get the money?"

Radiguet's jaw dropped. In his fury, his mad anxiety to kill the old man, he'd forgotten the other half, the most important half.

"Crease him, for Christ's sake," he responded angrily, "don't kill him."

"I thought maybe you wanted me to blow his belt buckle back about a foot."

"You hidin' behind a little girl, Radiguet?" Wayne Carrol's voice came from the street.

Radiguet turned and yelled, "You bring the payroll money?"

"They don't take that kind of money in hell, Radiguet," Wayne Carrol answered. "You won't need it."

As he saw Bletcher climb, still in his bare feet, over the barrels at the back door and toss the rifle onto the mud roof, following it on up using the barrels as a platform, Radiguet yelled, "I ain't goin' to shoot with you. That girl tore my hand with her teeth."

"You lyin' son of a bitch," Carrol called back, a hint of laughter in his voice. "Come on out here and play with me."

Wayne Carrol stood in the doorway of the restaurant, and behind him the population of Tres Cruces, armed only with machetes, waited.

They had brought the body of the sheriff inside, wrapped him in a sheet spread out on a table in the back, and they'd learned how deadly Shig Radiguet and Bletcher could be.

Wayne Carrol was even more knowledgeable than they about the pair he meant to face.

"I want both of you. Come out together."

"Bletcher's down," Radiguet yelled. "He took a batch of buckshot last night. It's you and me."

Chapo had already said that Bletcher had killed the sheriff, and that was after the shotgun had been uselessly fired. Fine. He's either on the roof or at the end of the street.

"Watch my back, Chapo," Wayne said softly to his friend. "The fat man will be somewhere."

"You got the payroll with you?" Shig yelled.

"Hell no!" Carrol shouted back. "Let's get on with it."

"You alone?" Radiguet stalled for time so that Bletcher wouldn't make a bad shot.

"I'm alone. Make your play. I ain't goin' to tell you again."

"What else you got in mind?" Radiguet laughed.

"I got it in mind to turn you over to the local citizens, while I just ride off and spend my money."

"I'm comin' out to parley. I'm comin' out with my hands up. I won't shoot with you with a bad hand."

"Bring the girl and turn her loose."

"Not till I have that payroll!" Shig roared, and strode out on the boardwalk with his hands raised.

Wayne knew what he was walking into, but he couldn't think of any other way to handle it so long as they had the girl.

The tall, gray-mustached man in clean blue jeans and chambray shirt stepped out into the street, his hand hovering over his holstered six-gun.

As dawn lighted the dusty little street, Carrol watched Radiguet warily and walked slowly toward him, waiting to hear a warning from Chapo.

"El techo!" came the cry. *"Allá!"*

Wayne Carrol raised his eyes but was a second

late before he caught sight of Bletcher lying flat on the roof to his left. Being right-handed, he had to swing to the left to make his shot, and it was that tiny delay that permitted Bletcher to squeeze the trigger on the heavy rifle before Carrol's bullet found his brain.

Wayne Carrol spun around from the force of the rifle bullet smashing through the muscle in his upper right arm, and the shock sent him to one knee. He had no idea where his six-gun had been flung from his paralyzed hand.

Fast as a cut cat, Shig Radiguet had his Colt in his hand and was advancing on the crowd.

"Get back!" Carrol called to Chapo.

"Move, you bastards!" Shig yelled, leveling the six-gun at Chapo, who crowded back into the restaurant with the others.

"Now, Mr. Highpockets, you ready to die?" Radiguet grinned down at Carrol.

"You won't kill me till you've got the money." Carrol spat on Shig's boot. "We both know that."

"Where is it?" Radiguet asked. "And no tricks. I got the girl."

"I need a guarantee you'll turn us all loose in exchange for the paybox."

"You got my word, and that's all." Shig kicked the older man in the belly to emphasize his words.

"No," Wayne Carrol choked out, as his lungs sought air.

"How far is the money?"

"Two hours."

"My deal is, she can ride behind you, with her hands loose to help you get along. That's it."

"And when I give you the box, you ride off and leave us."

"That's right. You're no worry to me anymore, old man," Shig Radiguet laughed.

Carrol knew the big man was lying, that they were likely riding off to their deaths, but he had to buy the time. Once up by Cache Valley, maybe his head would clear. Maybe there'd be a chance.

With the barrel of his Colt pressed against Wayne Carrol's head, Shig marched the older man over to the saloon and, inside, unpegged the door of the storeroom.

Maria stared at Carrol for a moment, noting the blood still dripping from his wounded arm, and got to her feet, whimpering.

"Calmate," Carrol said softly, and she held back from bolting.

"Out the back," Shig ordered, and once outside, cutting the bindings on her wrists, hoisted her up behind Carrol on Bletcher's horse.

"Nice . . ." Radiguet smiled as he felt her buttocks when he shoved her up.

"I've got your promise," Carrol said levelly.

"Sure, old-timer, lead off."

Carrol led them down the back alley and out of town onto the short plain.

The people of the town were like troops who

have lost their leader. Chapo tried to give them directions, but what could they do?

"Bring down the man," he yelled. "Bring his guns."

And after the people ran this way and that, finally three young men tumbled Bletcher's heavy body down onto the street and carried the rifle and the .45 as prizes, reluctantly passing them over to Chapo.

Chapo wanted to take his oldest son, but the boy was only eleven, so instead he chose the seventeen-year-old son of his sister.

"Can you fire the rifle?"

"Yes, of course," the boy said, but Chapo knew he was lying. There'd never been a repeating rifle in the village, and even he didn't fully understand it.

For that reason, he took the rifle and six-shooter and started off on his fastest Spanish mule after Shig Radiguet and his prisoners.

"*Coja es la pena, mas llega.*" Pain limps, but it arrives.

It was a punishing ride for Wayne Carrol. The girl riding behind him could feel the pain of his wound rack his body, and as they rode she undid the scarf from her shoulders and tied a sling around Carrol's neck, then lifted the arm gently and slipped it into the sling.

"*Gracias, chica,*" he murmured, glad that the ache was reduced.

What other way could he lead than toward his own people, who at least had a chance of defending themselves?

Shig Radiguet spurred his horse forward so that he was abreast of Carrol and the girl.

"This is the same trail I followed you on before. What are you trying to pull?"

"The money is up on the side of the mountain," Carrol said shortly. "You want it or not? It don't make a nevermind to me."

"You ain't entitled to any more mistakes, old man," Radiguet growled, and let his horse fall back a length so that he could watch the pair closely.

From the foothills, Carrol pointed the sorrel up the rocky trail towards Cache Valley.

"How much farther?" Radiguet called.

"Maybe three miles," Carrol replied. The pain in his arm had turned into a dull ache by now and his mind had cleared.

If he lost this game, he reflected, it would be because he'd been a hair slow in gunning Bletcher off the roof. That hair was the difference between live gunfighters and dead ones, and it was the reason he was in this jam right now.

Yet he saw it too as a bit of luck. Bletcher should have killed him, and ended the whole subject. The fact that he didn't sent a message loud and clear: You're too danged old to fight the top guns anymore.

Once you got that through your noggin, you could live until you fell off your horse.

It meant for him an end to rambling. He'd been ready for an ambush, but he'd still been late. Quit or die, old man, he told himself.

Once he had swallowed that ball of gristle, he felt free to attend to the immediate problem.

Not easy. That skunk was not only fast, he shot like he was down to his last cartridge.

The sorrel picked his way around the hairpins, steadily gaining elevation.

The best Wayne could think of was that when they all dismounted, he would charge Shig, catch him off balance, and maybe both of them would go over the cliff.

That'd get Maria loose.

Whether his brittle bones could stand that kind of a fall was open to argument.

They came to the bones of his good old horse, and Shig yelled happily, "That's that son of a bitch I killed last year."

Wayne shrugged his shoulders. What good could it do to call out insults to the hog-eyed man? He was too stupid to understand anything above the level of a skunk's butt.

At the fork, Wayne had to decide. He could turn left and lead them off on a false trail that would eventually end up over by Morenci, or he could turn right and lead the way to the pass into Cache Valley.

He guided the sorrel into the right, not knowing whether he was doing the right thing or not. He could go no faster than a walk on such a narrow, twisting trail, and there was no hope of somehow dodging, turning, or running away.

He thought about the best he could hope for would be a boulder dropping loose from above and landing on Shig Radiguet's head.

They finally came to the rock bench where the trail abruptly changed direction and slanted into Cache Valley.

"Hold it!" Radiguet yelled as the horse made the sharp left turn.

Even in that second there was still no chance, Wayne knew. Yes, he could kick the sorrel into a run and make a few yards, but you couldn't outrun a bullet.

Still, if Radiguet fired at them, they'd hear the shot down in the valley, an hour's ride away.

Add to that that Maria would be the one to catch the first bullet, and there wasn't anything to do except pull up.

"It's here," he said, and asked Maria to dismount. The bench was fifty yards around on a rough curve.

"Here?" Radiguet growled alertly.

"Just about," Carrol said, racking his brains.

Could he lead the dumb bastard on into camp? Not a chance. He wasn't that dumb.

"It's really my wife's money," Carrol said weakly, and then had the last-ditch solution

"Here's the deal," he said hurriedly before Radiguet could figure the cave's entrance was right under his nose. "I'm damaged, couldn't hurt a fly. Maria, she's no worry to you."

"So?"

"You set your guns back yonder. I'll give you the money and we'll leave whilst you count it."

"You think I'm crazy?" Shig laughed.

"It's the only way. If you kill us now, you get nothing. You let us go on, you get what you wanted."

"I don't trust you."

"Likewise, but it's the only way we can both have what we want."

"No, old man, I can smell that money! Where is it?"

"I told you how to get it."

"Now is when I start cutting up the top front of that little girl." Shig grinned. "Then you're going to screech like a treeful of owls."

Slipping the heavy bowie knife out of its sheath, Radiguet grabbed Maria by the hair and sliced the shirt and overalls down the center, partially revealing Maria's perfectly formed breasts, the nipples tiny and pink as Cecil Brunner rosebuds.

"Now, make up your mind, old man; where is it?"

"I guess you'd do it. I never knew a man so low."

Wayne made his way to the gash in the great rock and nodded. "It's in there."

"Bring it out," Radiguet said, suspiciously.

Wayne looked at Maria, murmured, *"No le hace,"* stepped into the cave, and looked around.

213

Gone. The money box was just plain flat out gone.

"Hurry it up!" Radiguet yelled.

"It's not here," Wayne called back. "Come and see for yourself."

"I knew you'd try a trick," Shig Radiguet roared, and forcing Maria to go ahead of him, he looked inside. "Where is it?"

"Chances are my dear little wife took it upon herself to keep it safe," Wayne said, a spark of humor in his eyes.

"Then where is she?" Radiguet demanded.

"I have no idea." Wayne shook his head. "She was talking about buying a hacienda in Mexico."

"Mexico? Goddamn you, Carrol, talk straight or . . ."

"Or?" came a young voice from behind a slab of rock. "Or what?"

Suddenly young Tyson emerged from his covert.

He was wearing the old patched-together Army .45 that had been on both sides of the Civil War before it was thrown away as broken, worn-out, and obsolete.

"Dang it, Tyson, get clear," Wayne gritted.

Shig wanted to draw, but he wanted to be sure of the money first. Hand hovering at his side, he said, "All I want is the payroll."

"There's no money in there. I just looked myself."

Tyson's cat eyes shone with cold concentration. "What the hell you mean, kid? Where is it?"

"I don't know where the money is, but you're on Cache Valley Ranch property, mister, and you ain't welcome," Tyson came back strongly.

"*Andale, chica,*" Wayne whispered, and gave Maria a little push to get her out of the line of fire.

"You damned snot of a kid," Shig growled. "I said get me the goddamned money, or I'm sluicing every one of you right now. . . ."

Before he'd finished speaking, his fingers had coiled around the butt of the .45 and had it on the rise when the boy suddenly dived to the ground, drawing as he fell. The move distracted Shig, who had planned to aim slightly upward at where the boy's eyes should have been; now he had to lower down again and catch the prone kid in his sights.

The old relic in the boy's hand exploded, black powder smoke erupted over the bench, and when Shig got his shot off, he was already spinning around. His bullet ricocheted off a rock, and the flattened lead cut through Wayne's upper leg, without, it seemed, hardly damaging him.

Shig stood staring at the boy, his pig eyes dull, his great chest heaving for breath, his barrel-like legs trembling.

He slowly lifted the .45, but before he could fire, Tyson shot him again and blew his belt buckle through his backbone.

Slowly Radiguet turned, pivoting on one foot, trying to keep his balance but slowly slipping one way, then the other, coming down a muscle at a

215

time until somewhere deep inside, his mind realized his life was gone, and from his hairy muzzle erupted a high, piercing scream ascending even as he fell into a quivering, kicking mass of nervous, dirty flesh, falling, shuddering, dying away, and the scream only ended in a drawn-out wheezing death rattle rising and falling.

Tyson saw the stubbled features change to the color of yellow clay; he smelled the stinking paunch of the gutshot mixed with sweet fresh blood, and he threw up.

Coughing and gagging, on hands and knees, he stared at the pool of vomit and knew he had done it.

"Son!" he heard his father call, but he wanted to hear nothing or say nothing. He just wanted to shudder and shake and retch up the sour bile.

"Son. If you don't mind," his father said mildly, "there's a lesson here I'd like you to learn."

"I learned my lesson, Dad—" the boy said, and heaved again.

"Not this one. Better hurry it up some."

The boy looked up and saw Maria with the bowie knife slicing open Wayne's pants leg, where a spurt of blood came squirting out regularly. His father's face was pale as he tried to undo the sling around his neck.

Tyson crawled over beside Wayne and said, "What is it, Dad?"

"This is the type of wound a man don't need,"

Wayne said patiently as Maria tried to stop the bleeding by pushing a balled-up bandanna onto the slitted wound.

The bright red blood came pumping out regularly despite the bandanna.

"Nicked an artery," Wayne said.

"Let me tie it up, Dad."

"First, listen to me. The way to stop the bleeding is to find a round pebble, then jam it in that cut, and then tie it in tighter'n hell so it blocks off the artery."

Wayne's face was pale as ocher limestone and his voice faded as Tyson scrambled around looking for a round pebble. One leaped into his hand, and in a second he had jammed it into the bleeding hole.

Quickly he cinched the scarf over it, bound it tightly in place, then, using a stick, he twisted the tourniquet down all the more. Miraculously the bleeding stopped.

"In about half an hour, let it off some, then lock her down again, until she quits. . . ." Wayne whispered.

"Yes, Dad," Tyson murmured as his father slipped into unconsciousness.

13

THE SPACIOUS UNFINISHED CABIN WAS FOUR logs high, founded on slabs of rock sledded down from the talus slope. The logs were of uniform size, trimmed and peeled to prevent the bugs from settling in.

In the past month, Kate had improved the camp so that each person had a deep pine-needle bed, and the general living area was shaded by a tarp soaked in linseed oil to make it rainproof. Log butts were used for chairs, benches, and side tables.

While able to get around some, Wayne Carrol wasn't permitted to mix in with the heavy work yet.

This Saturday morning, they had declared a day of rest, a time for cleaning up odds and ends, mending leathers, sharpening axes and the seven-foot crosscut saw they'd borrowed from Chapo.

The cabin would actually be two large spaces divided by a dog run and all covered by a pitched roof. The dog run could be closed in winter to make a mud room, or left open in the summer to make a breezeway.

Frank and Leonardo had bathed and put on clean outfits, oiled their hair after Kate had given them a trim with her sewing scissors, tied different-colored silk kerchiefs around their necks, Frank favoring a red polka dot, brushed their big hats, and were ready to leave.

Tyson seemed to have sprouted a couple of inches in the past few weeks, and Kate seemed to be putting on some extra tallow midways. But the main thing amongst them all was a feeling of contentment, the feeling that things were going good.

Weekdays they worked from dawn to dusk building the cabin and the corral, and they had no fears they couldn't finish the building in another month with plenty of time left to build more houses, or barns or springhouses, or tap into the hot spring they'd discovered back in a dogleg coulee.

"It'll never be any better'n right now." Wayne leaned back and inhaled the rich fragrance of the pines.

"Wait'll we get the training track built," Tyson said. "Then we'll have some fun!"

"Racin' those roans? I can't think of anything much better."

"That's all you think of," Kate said.

"I notice you been keepin' an eye on the ribby little filly."

"That filly will outrun any colt you can find in the cavvy," Kate declared. "I'll bet you."

"What'll you bet?" Wayne grinned.

"Sixty thousand dollars," Kate retorted.

"You bettin' my share too?" Frank smiled.

"Finders keepers," she teased.

"Girl, I'd like to a-peed when I seen that money box was gone," Wayne laughed, remembering back.

"Yes, and I liked to a-died that morning you run off again, and I found all them documents in your saddlebags. You're a dishonest man."

"Oughta be in jail," Frank said.

"Forged my name on the fee title," Leonardo said.

"Mine, too," Kate said.

"And mine too, and besides, he lied about my age," Tyson added.

"Well, I had a weak moment the first time I saw this place and I fell prey to temptation. I told the old devil to get behind me, but no, he puts a pen in my hand and says sign here and here and here and here five times."

"Up until you forged my name, Wayne, I always signed with an *X*." Frank chuckled. "Now I see it done official, maybe I can copy it."

"You boys always makin' fun, but I reckon if Tyson hadn't cut down on that big razorback, it'd gone for nothin'."

"What I learned that day," Tyson said slowly, digging a sliver out of his callused finger with his barlow jackknife, "was that I'd rather patch up hurt people than shoot 'em. Learning that trick of shuttin' off an artery seemed like it was ten times better'n how to draw and shoot."

"Likely we could use a doctor"—Kate smiled—"but I'm not sure you're the one for me."

"No, I want to ride the roans so long as my weight is down; after that, I'll just go along."

"Well, maybe by then your mind would be more settled to doctoring. God knows we got enough money to send you to school," Wayne said.

"We're going to take the young stud back east to Saratoga Springs," Tyson said. "We'll win everything they got."

"Take your time, Tyson; you already crowded in a couple lifetimes already," Kate said.

"I dunno. I want to work with the horses and race 'em, and prove we've got the best breed in the world since Justin Morgan, and then maybe I'd like to study up on medicine and such."

"Likely your dad'll be in South America or the North Pole by then," Kate said, "and I'll be scratchin' around here talkin' to the fence posts."

"No, child. This old hoss been broke to ride, and he ain't jumpin' no more fences."

"Oh, hell!" Kate shrieked. "Every time he starts talkin' that way, he's fixin' to run!"

"Got another hide-out valley in mind?" Frank asked.

"No, don't believe nothin' she says. She ain't been herself lately," Wayne protested. "I was thinkin' about that Saratoga Springs, I admit, and I was trying to figure how we could do better'n just win all the purses."

"What have you got in mind?" Leonardo asked,

running his finger inside his pink neckerchief. "Not that I want any part of it."

"They's a big, brand-new hotel there, and I mean they just wear diamonds big as horse buns, tryin' to show off their money, and I betcha Kate'd like a couple hatfuls of those diamonds, wouldn't you, Kate?"

"You listen to me, old-timer. . . ." She knelt in front of him and waggled her finger under his nose. "What I want is a straight up-and-down husband that'll be an example to his baby boy when he arrives."

"Oh, hell," Wayne said, "that shoots it."

"Reckon we'll be headin' out for Tres Cruces." Leonardo grinned. "Can't keep the ladies waitin'."

"What ladies?" Tyson asked, puzzled.

"Maria and her sister Josefina," Frank put in.

"Can I go along and leave these old folks to their own inventions?"

"I do believe there's another little sister," Leonardo said.

"Name of Paloma," Frank added.

"How old?" Tyson asked suspiciously.

"Oh, she's at least thirteen," Leonardo said.

"Just let me find my purple neckerchief and I'll be right with you." Tyson grinned.

Jack Curtis was born at Lincoln Center, Kansas. At an early age he came to live in Fresno, California. He served in the U.S. Navy during the Second World War, with duty in the Pacific theater. He began writing short stories after the war for the magazine market. Sam Peckinpah, later a film director, had also come from Fresno, and he enlisted Curtis in writing teleplays and story adaptations for *Dick Powell's Zane Grey Theater*. Sometimes Curtis shared credit for these teleplays with Peckinpah; sometimes he did not. Other work in the television industry followed with Curtis writing episodes for *The Rifleman, Have Gun, Will Travel*, Sam Peckinpah's *The Westerner, Rawhide, The Outlaws, Wagon Train, The Big Valley, The Virginian* and *Gunsmoke*. Curtis also contributed teleplays to non-Western series like *Dr. Kildare, Ben Casey* and *Four Star Theater*. He lives on a ranch in Big Sur, California, with his wife, LaVon. In recent years Jack Curtis published numerous books of poetry, wrote *Christmas in Calico* (1996) that was made into a television movie, and numerous Western novels, including *Lie, Eliza, Lie* (2002), *Pepper Tree Rider* (1994) and *No Mercy* (1995).

Center Point Publishing
600 Brooks Road ● PO Box 1
Thorndike ME 04986-0001 USA

(207) 568-3717

US & Canada:
1 800 929-9108
www.centerpointlargeprint.com